93

93

93

5

# A Fresh Wind
# in the Willows

by
## DIXON SCOTT

Illustrated by
*Jonathon Coudrille*

Heinemann/Quixote Press

For Helene

Heinemann/Quixote Press
10 Upper Grosvenor Street, London W1X 9PA

LONDON   MELBOURNE   TORONTO
JOHANNESBURG   AUCKLAND

Second impression March 1983

SBN:   434 98031 5

Printed in Great Britain by
St Edmundsbury Press
Bury St Edmunds, Suffolk

# Contents

# Mole's New Spring Fever

THE MOLE rested on his sculls and sighed a small, "O my!"
It wasn't the tired sigh of someone relieved at last of a taxing
chore; in fact, he had expended little energy on sculling,
doing no more than dip the blades into the water now and
then to keep the little blue and white boat bow-on as it flowed
along with the river.

It wasn't a sigh of despair either, for what was there to
be despairing about? All around spring was well aflame,
melting even the memory of winter's short, bare days and
long, imprisoning nights: birdsong gladdened the sun-kissed
air; bolting buds quickened the riverbank heartbeat; and
what breeze there was merely twinkled the fresh young
leaves at the very top of the willowgarth that bulged into
this stretch of the river, not causing even the tiniest ripple
on the water.

But it wasn't a sigh of contentment, and the Mole's fur
ruffled with embarrassment as his mind put words to the
cause of his restlessness.

"O my!" he murmured again, looking at the Water Rat.
"What an ungrateful animal I am; whatever will you think
of me?"

The Rat, seated cross-legged in the stern with his paws
clasped behind his head, snoozed on, as he had done for
the past ten minutes or more. His whiskers twitched
upwards on one side of his nose, then on the other; then

both lots of whiskers twitched up on both sides at the same time, turning his reposed visage into a smile as real river sounds and scents permeated the heavenly dream he was having about . . . being in a boat on the river.

The Mole coughed cautiously, hoping to waken his companion yet also hoping not to.

"Ratty! Er . . . Ratty, my dear friend."

The Rat opened one eye, kept it open for a second or two, then closed it again.

"Ratty," said the Mole, "I just wanted to talk to you about something."

"About what?" murmured the Rat, still half-asleep and wanting to be all-asleep.

"About our little boat – I mean *your* little boat."

"Wha'supwithit?" cried the Rat, leaping to his feet in a most landlubberly fashion and rocking the craft alarmingly as he searched around for evidence of damage or imminent disaster.

"O there's nothing up with it – I mean there's nothing *wrong* with it," the Mole hastened to assure him. "I just wanted to talk about it."

"Ah," said the Rat, greatly relieved at these words and immensely pleased, too. "O I see! But of course!"

He sat down again and stretched his arms and yawned deliciously into the sun.

"What a day, eh, Mole old chap? What a good-to-be-alive blessed day. What a day to be in this beautiful boat on this beautiful river. Go right ahead and expand on the joys of boating, you good fellow: pursue the subject to your heart's content – I understand, for as far as I'm concerned the next best thing to being in a boat is to talk about it."

The Mole opened his mouth to speak but lost heart. He lowered his face and stared at his feet and emitted another faint, "O my!"

The Rat gauged that his friend was temporarily overcome with emotion; so, understanding fellow that he was, he busied himself mopping up a few spots of moisture that had dripped inboard from the sculls, and untying a perfectly good knot on the lashing of a rope fender and re-knotting it, to give the Mole time to recover.

As he worked, he sang a ditty he had composed himself and seemed most appropriate to the occasion.

> "A boat is a sight to delight,
> It sits in the water just right.
> It ferries you hither
> It ferries you thither,
> Whatever may be re-qui-site.

*CHORUS* O give me a boat, any old boat,
> Narrow or broad in the beam.
> A schooner or scow, any old how
> As long as it's tight at the seam, the seam.
> As long as it's tight at the seam.
> A boat is a magical thing,
> It soars like a bird on the wing.
> It rolls and it wiggles
> It jibs and it jiggles,
> A jig-o-ling jollicking fling.
> O give me a boat, any old boat,
> Narrow or broad in the beam –"

The Rat broke off and said kindly: "I know umpteen verses, old chap; why don't you join in when it comes to 'O give me a boat, any old boat . . .'? That's the chorus, you see."

The Mole lifted his gaze from his feet.

"Ratty, you're such a *caring* person that I feel awful even mentioning it, I really do, but it's been niggling at me, it really has."

"Niggling at you?" said the Rat, taken aback. "What's been niggling at you?"

The Mole was silent again for almost a whole minute, obviously thinking deeply, while the Rat waited as patiently as he could, feigning preoccupation with other thoughts himself as animal etiquette demanded.

"The best way I can put it . . ." the Mole started at last, ". . . really the only way I can put it is: ice cream."

"Ice cream?"

"*Ice Cream!*"

"Well I never! Ice cream, eh?" chuckled the Rat. "Can't

7

help you there, old friend. If we'd brought any with us it would have been melted by now in any case.' Fraid you'll just have to let your niggle niggle on, unless – and it's hardly likely I must admit – unless we meet Mr Antonio pushing his barrow down the river! Besides," the Rat added in surprised tone, "you said you never wanted to see an ice cream again as long as you lived after last year's Vicarage Garden Fete!"

"That's what I mean, Ratty," the Mole said earnestly. "You remember they were giving away all the unsold ices at the end of the day because it would only be wasted otherwise, and I ate fifteen dishes of it and –"

"Sixteen! Come now, it was sixteen – most of them with several shakes of raspberry sauce on top."

"Fifteen!" insisted the Mole. "I didn't get two licks at the last one before I felt very queazy in my tummy and I didn't finish it, so that doesn't count. But I was very greedy, I admit."

"Innocence of youth," said the Rat comfortingly. "It was after all your very first encounter with ice cream. Perfectly understandable."

"And you pointed out, very *wisely* if I may say so, Ratty, that a fellow can have too much of a good thing."

"True, true," agreed the Rat, assuming a Badger-like gravity. "It's a very true saying, that one, always thought so."

The Mole trailed a paw in the water as he spoke again.

"Boating," he said. "We've been boating *every* single day, *all* day, for *four* whole weeks now."

The Rat, still preening at having been adjudged wise, failed at first to grasp the import of these words. When he did, an expression of pained incredulity spread over his handsome features. His eyes opened wide, his brow furrowed, his whiskers drooped and his jaw sagged.

"You mean . . . you don't mean you're tired of . . ." He struggled to get the word out, "of *boating?*"

The Mole turned to him quickly, almost tearfully.

"No, no Ratty, not *tired* of it, don't think that even for a moment! Dear me, of course not. I adore just messing about in this little boat as much as you do. It's just that, well, as you said, a fellow can get too much of a good thing."

It was the Rat's turn to bow his head, and the Mole, pained

8

with remorse, went on: "O please forgive me, Ratty, I didn't mean to speak like that, I don't feel like that at all really. I want things to go on just as before, so please forget I even *hinted* at being the *slightest* bit unhappy."

"Stop! Stop, dear Mole," said the Rat, holding up a paw, "I won't have you blaming yourself for my thoughtlessness. Humph! What a selfish creature I'm shown to be."

"O no, Ratty!"

"O yes! Here am I, a riverman born and bred, lamentably pursuing my own happiness, totally oblivious to the needs of a landsman like you – you who so selflessly abandoned your way of life for mine. To think that all this time the only concession I ever made to your instinct and desires was to share that memorable Christmas with you in your own dear cosy home –"

"Humble enough, Ratty."

" – while you fell into my ways so readily that I, in my arrogance, presumed it was the better life, the only life for us both."

The Mole protested: "But I love it, Ratty, honestly I love the way we live! Sometimes I wonder how I ever got by without knowing you and Badger and Toad and –"

He fell silent as an object whooshed over their heads and splooshed into the water alongside the boat; a round object that bobbed red and shiny on the surface.

"Goodness," said the Mole, "it looks like a cannonball! Are we being fired at, Ratty?"

The Rat reached over and scooped the object out of the river.

"Cannonballs don't float," he observed, wiping it dry with his drip rag, "but these do."

"What is it then?"

For answer the Rat stared up to the tops of the willows, from whence the object had descended.

"Mr. Toad himself, I'll be bound!"

"Toad?" queried the Mole in amazement. "What can it be to do with him?"

"Everything," said the Rat, "everything or nothing. My guess is – everything! Pull on those sculls, young Mole. Take us round the bend and we shall see."

9

"But what *is* it?" insisted the Mole, heaving away as the Rat began polishing the object on his forearm.

"You really don't know? Well, how odd! What this is, dear Mole, is the answer to your niggle! Haul away, my friend."

\* \* \*

The Mole sculled with vigour, splashing a good deal more than usual in his mounting excitement and sending the boat scudding round the willowgarth bend.

"Easy, old chap, or you'll run us aground," the Rat soon advised. "The clearing in the willows dead ahead – that's where we're making for."

He stepped past the Mole and got the painter ready, jumping ashore just before the boat touched and making fast to an overhanging bow.

"See now," he invited with a wave of his paw, "I was right. Toad it is!"

The Mole scrambled up the river bank and blinked and blinked and blinked again with pleasure at the strange and lively scene.

He and the Rat were on the edge of a lush green field of close-cropped grass. In the centre, a small army of stoats, weasels, hedgehogs and rabbits was heaving on a huge and heavy iron roller.

To the right of the field, verging a circling white line being freshly imprinted by a rabbit pushing what seemed like a tiny wheelbarrow with long handles, stood a pretty white pavilion with a green door and windowframes and a roof of reed thatch.

And alongside the pavilion in a practice net, immaculate in creamy pullover with green-edged v-neck, snow-white shirt and trousers, boots and pads and a bright green cap with the badge TH entwined in yellow, stood the impressive figure of Mr Toad of Toad Hall, facing up to a ball hurled down by a perspiring rabbit.

Toad swung his bat and despatched the ball into the air with a mighty thwack. The Mole and the Rat watched it soar over the trees and vanish, undoubtedly into the river.

"Bowl 'em faster, laddie!" Toad commanded the rabbit. "Increase your run-up and put more wrist action into your delivery. You've not tested me once yet!"

The rabbit mopped his brow and pointed out: "That's the seventh ball we've lost, Mr Toad, sir. Shouldn't we try to find some of them?"

"Waste of time!" Toad decreed. "I knocked 'em all into the next county; never find 'em in a month of Sundays. Plenty more where they came from anyway – I brought a gross with me. Bowl up now!"

The Rat shouted "Ahoy, there!" and threw the ball he had picked out of the river in Toad's direction. "That's one at least that didn't leave this county, Toady!"

Toad turned with a delighted "Hooray!" and a welcoming wave of his bat.

"Stout fellows, knew you wouldn't let me down! The Badger and Otter with you? No matter, they'll be along presently."

He put an arm around each of them and ushered them towards the pavilion.

"The togs are waiting for you in the changing rooms; bought out Sudbury's entire stock – cost a fortune fitting up two teams. Well worth it, though, good for the Toad Hall image, what! Community spirit and all that. You chaps are bound to find togs in your sizes if you nip in before I let the

11

Wild Wood oiks get at 'em. Only thing is, all the boots are Size 9, so wear two or three pairs of socks if you need to – plenty of *them*. Soon as you're kitted out, get yourselves over here to the net for a knock-up. I'll have this rabbit in some kind of shape by then. You bowl, Mole? Toss me a couple when you're ready – I warn you, though, I'm in cracking form."

The Mole looked bewildered as he and the Rat made their way into the pavilion and observed the handwritten notice on the door to the right saying, "Toad's Team", and another to the left saying, "Toad's Other Team." They opted for the room on the right and surveyed an array of pullovers, shirts, trousers, boots, pads and caps laid out in neat piles on the bench skirting the walls.

"What's it all about, Ratty?" the Mole enquired in his most perplexed voice. "Toad seemed to be *expecting* us."

"So he did," said the Rat. "That's because he *was* expecting us – to play cricket."

He tried on a cap that was so much too big that it hid his eyes and the peak came right down over his nose. The Mole couldn't help giggling as the Rat turned and said very loudly, "Howzat? Howzat?"

Pleased with the sound, the Mole repeated: "Howzat? Howzat?"

"That's what they're always yelling during a game of cricket," the Rat said. "Howzat? Howzat?"

"Why are they always yelling it, Ratty?"

"Why?" said the Rat, exchanging his cap for one that was just a bit too small. "Why? Because they're hoping the umpire will decree that the chap who's *in* is *out*, that's why!"

"O I see," said the Mole, not seeing at all really. He picked up a pair of trousers and stared at them blankly. "What's the chap who is *in* doing *in* and why do the others want him *out*?"

A dazed expression came over the Rat's face.

"You mean to say, Mole, you don't know anything at all about cricket?"

"No," admitted the Mole very apologetically.

"Well I'm blessed – and you an Englishman! Nothing to the game really. One team goes *in* to bat and whack the

ball and score runs while the team that's not *in* bowls the
ball trying to hit the stumps of the chaps who *are* in and
put 'em *out*. When the chaps who are *in* are all *out*, the
other team goes *in* for their whack and if they can whack
up more runs before they're *out* than the other chaps did
while *they* were in, they're the winners. Got it?"

"Yes, I think so," said the Mole, not wishing to appear
unintelligent. He added anxiously: "Does it hurt when they
hit your stumps, Ratty?"

"Only your pride," said the Rat, holding a shirt up to the
Mole's chest. "That'll do for you, I think."

"It sounds fun," said the Mole, still looking puzzled.

He put on three pairs of socks to take up some of the space
left by his Size 4 feet inside the Size 9 boots. Even three pairs
weren't nearly enough, but no amount of tugging and pulling
could force another sock over the others.

"What I can't understand," he said, "is how Toad was
expecting to see us if we weren't expecting to see him."

The Rat, clumping unsteadily up and down the pavilion
floor trying to get the feel of his own oversize boots, informed
him: "But we were, old chap – at least *I* was. I decided to let it
come to you as a surprise."

"Aaaaagh," went the Mole very expressively. "I understand
now. O yes, I see now. You *forgot*, did you?"

"Not at all!" said the Rat. "Well – perhaps I tried to forget.
Frankly Mole, I didn't tell you about this proposed encounter
in the hope that when we got here the whole thing would
have been called off. All Toad's grand ideas have a weak spot
– usually it's Toady himself. We may be sorry at the end of
the day that we took any part in this affair."

"But surely there's no harm in just playing a game, Ratty.
What can possibly go wrong when you're only playing?"

"What can possibly go wrong, dear Mole, has already been
hinted at: Oiks. You heard Toad say it – a most insulting term
and he used it in reference to the Wild Wooders. This is
supposed to be a *friendly* match; Toad dreamt up the idea in
the fond belief it would further good relations between the
Riverbank and Wild Wood communities. And then he has to
go and call them oiks! If they hear him . . . if Badger hears
him, O dear!"

13

"O dear indeed," said a gruff, unmistakable voice. "If I hear *what*, Ratty?"

The Badger had appeared at the door of the changing room with as little heraldry as the Riverbanker at his side, Otter.

With an urgent wink in the Mole's direction the Rat explained he was just a little worried that all would not go as well as intended because Toad was already being a bit too boastful.

"Just being his natural self, eh?" observed Otter. "I shouldn't have come: didn't like the prospect from the start, like it less now. The leopard can't change his spots, Toad can't change the thickness of his skin. Think I'll be off."

"Hold hard, hold hard," commanded the Badger, lifting a long white coat from a hook on the wall and looking the others seriously in the eye in turn.

"Now then, I know Toad, you know Toad, we all know Toad: a broad-hearted fellow full of good intentions that now and then don't turn out good. Sometimes it's his fault and sometimes it ain't. Sometimes it's the fault of his friends for not giving him firm guidance."

The Badger donned the white coat and began buttoning it up with such deliberation, while still looking sternly at the others, that they all knew not to speak because he had more to say yet.

When the last button was button-holed, he continued: "There now, you see before you an umpire; that's my role on this occasion. My fellow umpire will be the Chief Weasel and fair play is what we both intend to ensure without fear or favour. You have my assurance that the event about to take place will be so firmly under control that not even a regiment of boastful Toads could cause the slightest trouble."

Before anyone else could speak a thunder of stampeding paws engulfed the pavilion and the changing room was invaded by rabbits, weasels, stoats and hedgehogs pouncing on the piles of togs.

The Badger reached out and seized the ear of a rabbit who was tugging with a stoat for possession of a sweater.

"What's all the rush, my lad?" he admonished. "Where are your manners?"

"Please, sir," said the rabbit, "Mr Toad said everyone who managed to get kitted out could play in the match. Let me go, sir, I've been practising bowling harder than anyone else and it would be rotten unfair if this Wild Wood oik got to play instead of me."

"*What?*" bellowed the Badger, "this Wild Wood *what* did you call him?"

"Mr Toad calls them that, sir, and he's a real gentleman so it must be all right," said the rabbit.

He executed a swift tug-and-swerve manoeuvre that simultaneously freed his ear from the Badger's grasp and the sweater from the stoat's grasp, then dived into a melee of other animals wrestling for possession of boots.

The Rat, seeing the Badger's face darken, said apologetically: "I'm afraid that what the rabbit says is true, Badger, but I don't think Toad meant it –"

"Oiks!" exploded the Badger, "Oiks! Oiks, eh? Dear me! Oiks of all things! Gentlemen, I fear this match may be more difficult to control than I had bargained for. Let us without delay proceed to lay down the umpire's law to foolish Toad."

In the centre of the field, as the Badger approached with the Rat, the Mole and Otter in close support, Toad was making a great show of apparently inspecting each blade of grass and sniffing the air.

"Mmmm," he murmured before they were within earshot, gazing over their heads at the sky, "it's a bowler's dream of a wicket. If I win the toss I'll put 'em in first and skittle 'em out in no time. On the other hand, if I skittle 'em out with nothing on the scoreboard – as I certainly shall – I won't have cause to knock up a century or two – as I certainly should. The thing to do undoubtedly is to make it a two-innings game, two innings for *them*, that is. Then I can put 'em in to bat first and shatter 'em with my magnificent bowling and then go in and notch up a huge total with superb batting and declare the innings then put 'em in again and skittle 'em out and –"

"Toad," said the Badger, "I want a word with you!"

"O hello, you chaps!" Toad greeted them. "I was just ruminating on this glorious game we call cricket . . . the essence of sportsmanship . . . the spirit of England itself . . .

'The game's afoot . . . Cry God for Harry! England and Saint George!'"

"Toad," repeated the Badger through gritted teeth, "I want a word with you. I am most disturbed at a suggestion that you have been using a dergo- . . . a drego- . . ."

"A derogatory expression," said the Rat helpfully.

" . . . a nasty word to describe the Wild Wooders," went on the Badger, "of whom, I would remind you, I am one."

"Me?" said Toad in genuine astonishment. "I used a nasty word about *you*, Badger? Never! Why, you're the most splendid chap I know –"

"The word," continued the Badger, "was oiks – and you used it."

"O that," said Toad, turning crimson. "A slip of the tongue, mere figure of speech. If I said it – and I certainly don't remember ever saying it – I certainly didn't mean it to include you, old chap."

"You'd better not to have meant it to include *anyone*, you wretched Toad! Wild Wooders might not all always act as gentlemanly as we might expect of them, we all of us know that, but there's nothing more calculated to bring out the vicious ruffian in 'em than to hear themselves called what you called them. You are a silly, thoughtless, unspeakable cad!"

Toad squirmed under the Badger's lashing, feeling how unfair it was to find himself in such a humiliating position after spending so much money on the togs and so much time arranging this unique social occasion.

The Rat and the Mole and even Otter began to feel rather sorry for him when the Badger thundered: "I've a mind to call the Chief Weasel over and advise him to abandon this event here and now because of your shameful attitude!"

Toad turned with a wild look of pleading in his eyes to the others to save him from such public degradation, and Otter, as the Rat and the Mole nodded in urgent support, urged: "Please, Badger, give him another chance."

"Well," growled the Badger, "do we have your solemn oath as the gentleman you *can* be, Toad, that the vile word in question will not pass your lips – nay, never even enter your head again?"

"O quite," said Toad with a choke in his voice and a dejected wave of his paw. "O indeed . . . solemn oath . . . as a gentleman . . . goes without saying."

The Badger seemed to take an eternity coming to a decision and everyone looked in every direction other than at each other, and especially not at Toad, as they waited.

"In that case," the Badger pronounced at last, "the match may commence."

# The Cricket Match

IT WAS a subdued Toad who called "Heads" when the Chief Weasel spun a coin that came down "Tails", giving the captain of Toad's Other Team, a stoat who had been making some deft strokes with the bat in the practice net, the choice of batting or bowling first.

Toad smiled wryly as the stoat opted to bat; with a humble "Thank you, sir," he accepted the ball proffered by the Chief Weasel, sighed deeply for all around to hear, as if reconciled already to losing the match having lost the toss, and set off at a forlorn, droop-shouldered trudge to pace out his bowling run-up. On and on he went, long past the point where even the fastest bowler would make his mark; on and on to the very boundary line itself, where two rabbits who had settled themselves at a narrow angle to the wicket, the better to observe the niceties of attack and defence, became so alarmed at his changing appearance as he approached that they leapt up and scuttled to the safety of the numbers sprawled near the pavilion.

Toad had taken on a countenance so fiendish that horns seemed even to sprout from his head and smoke to snort from his nostrils. On the boundary line he executed a ritual of whirling his right arm like a catherine wheel while running on the spot with a tattoo of steps of such intensity he might have been drumming up dark forces from the nether regions to power his cause.

Then he turned and steamed like an express locomotive towards the wicket to inflict his terrible onslaught on whoever was the unfortunate batsman taking guard: the Rat, as it turned out.

The Rat, Otter and three other Riverbankers had been assigned to the Wild Wood side and five stoats and weasels to the Riverbank team to underline the friendliness of the encounter; whatever the outcome, no one would be able to say the Wild Wooders had actually won or the Riverbankers had actually won. On the other hand, everyone would be able to return home to the Riverbank or the Wild Wood happy in the knowledge they hadn't actually lost: a Solomon-like arrangement for which Toad, as he thought it up himself, deserved full praise – were it not for the fact that he secretly intended to emerge basking in praise as the hero of the match on either side.

The Rat gulped and patted the ground nervously with his bat as he watched Toad's fiery approach. The ball was indeed almost as hard as the cannonball the Mole had mistaken it for, and if he got in the way of it with his body instead of with his bat . . .

Now Toad, reaching the point of delivery, unleashed the

ball with the near velocity of a cannon shot, then tripped trying to arrest his own momentum and fell on his face, expelling air like a burst balloon. He looked up, expecting to see the Rat's stumps splayed in all directions, but saw instead the Rat and everyone else staring skywards at the ball now vanishing over the willows and undoubtedly into the river.

"Good shot, Ratty old chap," gasped Toad in genuine admiration. "Don't know how you managed it, dashed if I do!"

"*He* didn't, *you* did, Toad," said the Badger, signalling to the pavilion where a hedgehog was keeping score. "You threw it all that way without touching the ground. That's six runs to them."

The Badger produced another ball from his pocket.

"That one," he said, nodding at the trees, "can be regarded as lost. Try not to be so extravagant, Toad."

"Hummmph!" said Toad. "It seems I may have misjudged the wicket – not, of course, that I'd be the first captain to be so deceived. In all probability there's a fine line here between a fast bowler's paradise and a slow bowler's paradise; let us now determine the truth. Badger – Mr Umpire, that is – I shall now abandon the pace ball for a slow off-spin delivery."

"So be it," said the Badger in gritted monotone, "bowl whichever way you wish as long as the ball arrives at the other end within reasonable striking distance of the batsman, that's all we ask."

This time Toad executed no more than a hop, skip and a jump before sending the ball bouncing gently in the direction of the Rat, who promptly smacked it for six.

Toad thereupon clutched his left leg and fell to the ground moaning, "O my ankle!"

Everyone gathered around, rather mystified but trying to help as he writhed in seeming agony.

"I've twisted it badly," blurted Toad. "O dear, I fear it's the end of my bowling for now. I'll leave the field and rest for a while. If a couple of chaps could give me a hand . . ."

The Mole and a stoat readily obliged and Toad, grimacing and emitting small cries of pain and somehow managing to look pale and brave, leaned heavily on their shoulders as he hobbled towards the pavilion.

The Badger, at least, noticed that Toad limped sometimes with his left foot and sometimes with his right, as if he couldn't remember which ankle he'd twisted.

"Mole," said Toad as he sank heavily to a bench outside the pavilion, "you must take over as Captain until I've recovered."

"Me?" said the Mole, wide-eyed. "But Toad, I don't know how to be a Captain, I've never even –"

"Don't worry, dear fellow, old Toad will be here helping you to cope. I'm afraid the runs are going to come thick and fast while I'm not out there to prevent it, but if you put that rabbit on to bowl, the one I was instructing when you arrived, he may put up some kind of resistance until I'm fit to step back into the breach."

When the game resumed the Badger informed the rabbit bowler that as Toad had delivered one no-ball there were still five to go to complete the first over.

"Thank you, sir," said the rabbit, laying his ears flat so he wouldn't hear much if the Badger referred again to the sweater-tugging incident, "I'll do my best, sir."

He walked only half a dozen paces, polishing the ball on his trouser leg, then returned in two bounds and with a splendid wrist action sent it down the pitch so swiftly and accurately that the Rat blinked and missed it: the ball thumped one of his leg pads and immediately the rabbit and several others in his team leapt into the air shouting "Howzat?" "Howzat?"

"Out!" ruled the Badger, "Leg Before Wicket."

The Rat grinned and walked from the field, handing his bat to Otter, next at the wicket.

"You certainly knocked that rabbit into shape," the Rat said, sitting next to Toad and taking off his pads.

"Yes, he's a promising lad," Toad said in a grand manner. "I may be able to make something of him given time. Shall we say he's having a bit of beginner's luck –"

He stopped speaking as Otter started walking from the crease, the stumps rattled behind him.

"Mind you," continued Toad, "it looks as if it's become a true bowler's wicket since I began the taming of it."

There followed an amazing twenty minutes, during which the rabbit sent the next three batsmen packing and then, after

Captain Mole's reasonable plea to the umpires – without consulting Toad – that as the team had no other bowler available because of injury the rabbit should be allowed to continue his attack from the other end, the rampaging rabbit despatched the remainder of Toad's Other Team without a run being added.

Toad quickly buckled on leg pads as the players trooped off the pitch, an exultant cohort carrying the rabbit shoulder-high.

"Mole," called Toad, making imaginary strokes at an imaginary ball with an imaginary bat and ignoring the triumphant rabbit, "get yourself padded up, laddie! Twelve all out, eh? We've not much of a target to go for but it's obviously the stickiest wicket a batsman could ever encounter – amazing how conditions change from one moment to the other. You and I will open the batting for Toad's Team and demonstrate how skill and courage can carry the day."

The Mole peered at Toad's feet: he was dancing agilely from one to the other as he swung his imaginary bat, as if oblivious to the pain that had forced his early retirement as a bowler.

"But your ankle, Toad," said the Mole. "Are you sure you're fit to carry on?"

"O that!" said Toad, interrupting his miming performance to lift his left leg with a small wince, then changing his mind and wiggling his right foot. "Scarcely any pain at all now. What there is I shall just have to put up with – it's the game that counts, not poor old Toad and his misfortunes."

He lowered his voice like a conspirator.

"Now here's my plan of campaign, old chap; tactics, you understand. At the moment we don't know the strength of their bowling and it's vitally important that we do – at least it's vitally important that *I* do. So I want you to receive the first over."

"Me?" said the Mole in even more alarm than when he had been appointed Captain. "But Toad, you're such a splendid batsman and I've never even held a bat before and –"

"That's just it, Mole! It won't matter if you lose *your* wicket, but as I'm the one who's going to have to make all the runs and save the day, it won't do if by some accident or

22

weaselly trick I'm put out before I've a chance to assess what they're capable of. Just try to keep your end up until I get into my stride and there'll be no stopping me, you'll see."

So the Mole, feeling very lonely and inadequate as members of Toad's Other Team crowded close in around him, poised to seize upon his slightest slip, took guard and prepared to defend his wicket from a stoat who was limbering up at the other end almost as spectacularly as Toad had done.

"O my," thought the Mole as the stoat began his pell-mell approach. He saw the ball leave the stoat's grasp and streak towards him; he closed his eyes and stuck out his bat, heard the snick of leather on willow and opened his eyes to see Toad leaping down the pitch yelling, "Run!"

The Mole scuttled towards Toad's end, with the ball still bouncing to the outfield and three Wild Wooders in pursuit, and Toad called as they passed one another: "Two in this easily!"

But the Mole, dazed with the realisation he had made his first run, was in no mood to put himself immediately back into the firing line; he stayed firmly in the sanctuary of the bowler's end of the pitch, thus forcing Toad, already bounding along for a second run, to scramble back a split second before the returned ball lifted his bails.

"Ratty," the exultant Mole called to the Water Rat, who was positioned nearby as a fielder, "I've scored a run! Me, Mole – I've scored a run!"

"Well done!" the Rat congratulated him. "I'm proud of you."

The Mole couldn't contain his excitement. He spotted Otter in the outfield.

"Otter!" he shouted. "I scored a run – me, Mole!"

The Otter grinned and waved and called back: "More than I did!"

The Mole looked around for any other friendly face to share his joy.

"Badger, Badger! Did you see – I scored a run!"

The Badger permitted himself the suggestion of a smile.

"Stout fellow, well played. Let us see if Toad can emulate you."

"O he will, he will!" cried the Mole, his chest heaving with emotion. "Toad's so splendid at it. But me . . . just fancy me scoring a run!"

He was still dancing around in heady delight when the Chief Weasel, not unkindly, asked him to move to one side and remain still so that the stoat could resume the bowling – with Toad now on the receiving end.

The stoat came loping and buckling along, as stoats do, but sent a ball to Toad that was not very fast, not very accurate and not very missable: in fact, it could have been judged wide and the Chief Weasel was about to rule so as Toad attempted to swipe it into the next county. The ball hit his left pad.

Immediately the Mole, throwing himself utterly into the spirit of his exciting new game, shouted, "Howzat! Howzat!" in the Rat's direction.

The stoat bowler was taken aback momentarily. He was aware that Toad's leg had stopped the ball, and he was equally aware that in no way had Toad's leg stopped the ball from hitting the stumps; but natural guile impelled him to take advantage of the situation and he swung his arms skywards as he turned to the Chief Weasel and appealed: "How *was* that?"

"Out," ruled the Chief Weasel.

"What?" called Toad. "What do you mean, *out?*"

"Out!" said the Chief Weasel.

"*I'm not!*" screamed Toad, advancing down the wicket waving his bat. "That ball was a mile off the stumps – it wouldn't have hit them in a month of Sundays!"

"Out!" insisted the Chief Weasel. "Don't argue with the umpire, Mr. Toad. Your own team-mate agrees – he was the first to acknowledge you were Leg Before Wicket."

"O my," said the Mole, "I really didn't mean –"

"Mole doesn't know anything at all about cricket!" shouted Toad, leaping up and down with rage. "It's ludicrous!"

"At least he's scored a run, which is more than you've done," observed the stoat bowler. "Start walking, Mr Toad."

Dazedly Toad took a few steps towards the pavilion, then changed his mind.

"I *won't*, I *won't!*" he sobbed, turning purple. "They're *my* bats and *my* balls and *my* stumps and *my* togs and it was *my* idea and . . . and . . ."

*Immediately the Mole shouted, "Howzat! Howzat!"*

He suddenly swung his bat about him viciously as if it were a club.

"You're all OIKS, the lot of you!" he shrilled. "OIKS! OIKS! OIKS! The Wild Wood is full of OIKS!"

This final outburst stunned everyone on the field, including the Rat, the Mole and Otter and particularly the Badger. Then every Wild Wooder was galvanized into snarling fury: from all directions they rushed in on Toad, swinging feet and fists at him with passionate abandon.

The embattled animal conducted himself with courage born of anger for a few seconds, scything the air with the bat to keep his assailants at bay. But the odds were overwhelming and as his courage ebbed he turned tail, burst out of the encircling mob and fled in panic round the field with the Wild Wooders in full cry after him.

The Badger was first among Toad's friends to react to his plight. Snatching out two stumps and brandishing one in either hand, he charged after the pursuers yelling, "Hang on, Toad, help is at hand!"

The Rat also seized two stumps, Otter a third, and together they pounded across the field in the Badger's wake, whirling their makeshift staves, followed by the Mole wielding his bat like a battleaxe; all of them intent on the immediate need to save Toad's skin, but all of them convinced that Toad deserved punishment for his shameful behaviour.

They managed to head off Toad after he had completed a near-circuit of the field, and interposing themselves between him and the howling Wild Wooders they swung their weapons threateningly, though taking care not to strike any actual blows, covering his retreat to the pavilion.

There all five took refuge in the dressing room marked Toad's Team and the Badger leant on the securely bolted door, getting his breath back as Wild Wooders hammered on it and fierce faces pressed at the window baying anger.

Amid the din the Badger pointed a stump at Toad cowering in the farthest corner.

"Wretched animal!" he gasped. "Unworthy son of a father . . . I held in such respect . . . you've done it this time and no mistake!"

He flung the stump to the floor in exasperation and it

bounced across the room and smacked against the wall quite close to Toad now almost petrified with fear and shame. Toad's plump body quivered in spasms and his eyes opened fleetingly, rolling in terror and closing again to shut out the unacceptable truth of his present position.

The Mole hung his head low between his knees and concentrated on unfastening his leg pads as he said: "If I hadn't shouted when I did, poor Toad wouldn't have acted as he did and –"

But the Badger waved him into silence.

"There can be no justification, no excuse, none at all," he decreed.

He placed himself four-square in front of the window, wearing a fierce scowl, at which the threatening faces outside were drawn back a yard or two, such was the healthy respect for his fighting qualities even from behind the shield of glass, but the shrieking and baying continued.

"How on earth are we going to pull Toad out of this hole?" he said. "They want justice – but what form of justice would suffice? They have right on their side – but we can't deliver Toad up to mob law."

The Rat said: "Perhaps if we all of us apologised on Toad's behalf, saying how terribly sorry and ashamed we were –"

"Not good enough," said the Badger, "words just won't be good enough; deeds is what will count now, not words."

"How about," suggested Otter, "if Toad made a gift of all this cricket gear to the Wild Wooders? It cost a lot and though they'll not be in a hurry to play with us again, they'd probably be pleased to have games among themselves."

"Could help, that," said the Badger. "But Toad wouldn't really have paid for his iniquity, would he? Mere out of pocket expenses to him, wouldn't feel a thing."

No one could think of any other suitable recompense and the Mole was about to suggest he start digging an escape tunnel under the pavilion floor, which he knew he would be better at than anyone else, when the Badger said musingly: "I wonder . . . now, I just wonder –"

Turning to the others the Badger drew himself up to his full height. "I shall go out and parley with the Chief Weasel," he announced solemnly. "Be sure to lock the door behind me."

27

"O Badger," said the Mole, "is it safe for you to do that – alone, I mean?"

"Safe for me but for no one else, I think."

The Rat, Otter and Mole gathered at the window and watched the noble Badger stride resolutely out into the sunshine through the parting ranks of Wild Wooders and approach the Chief Weasel with outstretched paw, much to that worthy's unease. The Badger put an arm around the Chief Weasel's shoulder and walked him off along the cricket pitch boundary line.

There was silence now as all inside and outside the pavilion waited on the outcome of this development.

Toad, emerging from his deep shock, uttered shakily: "Have they all gone? Is it all over?"

"I'm afraid not, old chap," said the Rat. "Badger's out there with the Chief Weasel, deciding your fate."

"Ooooo," moaned Toad, closing his eyes again.

As the two umpires continued their perambulation, the Chief Weasel could be seen waving his arms about from time to time, even pointing back at the pavilion and shaking a paw in emphatic gestures.

"It doesn't look very promising," said the Otter, a comment that drew more moaning from Toad.

On and on went the two figures, and when they had reached the farthest point from the watchers on their circular course it seemed that the Chief Weasel's manner had changed; no more was he gesticulating; it appeared he was even laughing, as indeed proved the case as he and the Badger suddenly turned and headed straight back across the field to the pavilion.

"Well, they're both all smiles about something," the Rat said with relief. "I wonder what brought that about?"

On reaching the pavilion the Badger and the Chief Weasel took up commanding positions on the steps, and the Badger called for Toad to be produced.

Toad forced himself to his feet – or rather to a foot, wincing as he resumed his limp – and the Rat and Otter shouldered him out like a wounded soldier being helped back from the front line.

"They wouldn't attack an injured animal, would they?" he beseeched them.

"No one's going to attack you now," Otter assured him, but Toad kept up his limp as a precaution as they moved outside.

They stood, all three, on the top step, flanked by the Chief Weasel and the Badger, and the Badger began to speak.

"Fellow Wild Wooders, fellow Riverbankers, fellow *creatures*," he enunciated with great deliberation . . . and a cheer went up in acknowledgement.

"One among us here today has been recklessly offensive. I will not dwell on how he has been offensive, for we all of us know that a slander repeated can reopen a wound already begun to heal . . ."

Cries of "Here, here!" but a lot more of "Shame!" interrupted the Badger's oration.

"Standing before you is a deeply remorseful Toad who bitterly regrets his indiscretion . . . he will tell you so. Carry on, Toad."

Toad gulped and rolled his eyes at the sky.

"Bitterly remorseful . . . deeply regret . . . most terribly sorry," he stammered.

"Apologies aren't enough!" yelled a Wild Wooder, and other voices took up the cry.

"They are not enough and nor are they intended to be enough," went on the Badger. "Firstly, Mr Toad has agreed to make token amends by bequeathing all his new and splendid collection of bats, balls and togs to the Wild Wood Cricket Club, which is here and now established."

A cheer went up, drowning Toad's relieved, "Pleasure, pleasure, I'm sure . . ."

"Secondly, and more importantly," continued the Badger, with a wink at the Chief Weasel, "we come to Mr Toad's real penance."

He paused like an actor timing his most dramatic lines, waiting for the last shuffle and cough from the audience to be suppressed.

Then: "Immediately I have finished speaking," the Badger's voice rang out, "Mr Toad will take urgent steps to hire a charabanc that will, tomorrow morning at eight o'clock precisely, pick up as many Wild Wood young 'uns as can be packed into it and take 'em off for a day at the seaside."

Another great cheer went up, again drowning Toad's

equable "Pleasure, pleasure . . . happy to do it . . ."

"Furthermore, Mr Toad himself, he alone with no other to turn to for succour or aid, will accompany these young ones and ensure they have a splendid outing and return safely to their homes in good time for supper.

"My friends (and here the Badger shook his head in a gesture of deep sadness, as if contemplating unbearable suffering) my friends, those hours of anguish between the setting off in the morning and the arrival home at night are not ones I would seek to endure myself; rather I would lock my door and hibernate for the summer as well as the winter.

"There will be on the cheeks of those dear little ones numerous tears, because the sun is too hot and burning them or the sea is too cold and freezing them; Mr Toad will have the drying of those tears. There will be tears because someone has trampled their sandcastle or they've buried their bucket and spade and forgotten where; all down to Mr Toad. Tears because 'Mr Toad, I've lost a shoe!' or 'Mr Toad, I've lost a sock!' or 'Mr Toad, someone's kicking sand in my eyes!' Tears because guzzled dishes of cockles and winkles and whelks and other salty things don't go down well with irresistible ice creams and sticky sweet things, and don't *stay* down after incessant rides on chairoplanes and swings and roundabouts; Toad won't have a hanky left for his own tears. Young 'uns will be crying because they've wandered off and got lost, crying because they've fallen while paddling and soaked their trousers, crying because a crab's pinched their toe, crying because Punch has hit Judy or the crocodile has eaten whoever he eats; crying because 'Mr Toad, I'm tired and want to go home!' and crying because 'Mr Toad, I don't want to go home!' And it will undoubtedly rain most, if not all, of the time.

"At the end of the day, when all the young Wild Wooders are back home and tucked up in bed, they will tell their doting parents they've had the happiest, most excitingest day of their lives . . ."

The Badger paused again.

"But Mr Toad won't be able to say that, will he?"

The silence seemed to become even deeper as the Badger finished describing the terrible penalty Toad was to pay for his sin.

30

Then the Chief Weasel began a grin that seemed eventually to stretch even beyond his ears.

"No," he said, "Mr Toad will certainly *not* feel he has had a happy day! Let's give him three cheers, lads, for being such a good sport! Hip-hip-hip –"

Toad didn't hear even the first exultant hooray: he had collapsed in a heap, all of a faint.

\*　　\*　　\*

"Ratty," the Mole called from his bed, "I feel *awfully* sorry for poor Toad, don't you?"

"Yes," the Rat murmured drowsily, wondering how many more times the Mole was going to say how sorry he was for Toad and how many more times he was going to have to say yes.

"What an *awful* punishment, isn't it? Awful . . . I never want to go to the seaside, do you Ratty?"

Hearing nothing for several moments, the Mole repeated: "Do you, Ratty – ever want to go to the seaside?"

"Hope I never have to," was the faint discouraging response.

"Ratty, about cricket . . ."

"O must we talk about it now, old chap?"

"No, no, not at all, Ratty. Dear me, no, not at all. I was just wondering though, were *you* ever captain of a team?"

"No, Mole, can't say I ever was. The opportunity never arose for me like it did for you today. You did splendidly."

"Thank you, Ratty."

The grandfather clock ticked soothingly on and the Rat was verging into a beautiful dream about being on the River, when the Mole spoke again.

"Ratty, cricket's all right once in a while – but let us spend every day on the river from now on, shall we?"

"You're very kind, dear friend," said the Rat, rousing himself, "so thoughtful. We'll do other things sometimes, though. New experiences are good for the soul; make you appreciate what you've got."

"How true that is, Ratty, how true . . ."

The Rat began drifting off again into blessed river-borne oblivion and he couldn't swear afterwards that he heard a

31

small voice murmuring in sleepy tones of wonder: "One, not out! Me . . . *Captain* Mole . . . One, not out! Howzat! Howzat! O my . . ."

# Toad's Flight of Fancy

THE BADGER couldn't believe his ears when the news was brought to him on a relay system that began with a heron who could hardly believe his eyes.

The heron, dropping a newly-caught roach in astonishment, had winged down river open-beaked at – for him – a very fast flap indeed to find someone, anyone, to tell him what he thought he might have seen.

Otter, distracted by the heron's agitated approach, let a juicy eel slip by; he stayed on the surface listening to the bird's babbling, eventually dipped underwater to collect his thoughts and then, as could be judged by the departing line of bubbles, sped on down river to the Water Rat's home.

The Rat and the Mole, much perturbed by the Otter's tidings, had set off at a run without further ado (not that they had been ado-ing anything other than sit back reading the morning papers, amid the debris of the breakfast table, when Otter launched in upon them) and they puffed and panted all the way to the Wild Wood and onwards into the heart of it, gathering a train of excitedly curious stoats and weasels in their wake as they made for the Badger's front door.

Now the Badger stood beslippered on his doorstep, having heard the Rat's breathlessly imparted intelligence, punctuated by the Mole's "O my, surely Toad must be ill!"

"What!" said the Badger. "Stuff and nonsense! Whoever heard of a flying Toad?"

"According to Otter," puffed the Rat, "the heron said Toad was cavorting about his lawn, flapping his wings – I mean arms – and leaping into the air, wearing a sort of suit made of feathers."

"And with what looked like a *beak* fixed to his nose!" added the Mole in amplification. "And an enormous tail!"

"It sounds foolish enough," said the Badger, "and also harmless enough, so I'm inclined to –"

"But, Badger, the last sight the heron had was of Toad climbing a tree . . . and if he . . . if he intends to –"

"To jump?" said the Badger. "O my sainted aunt! Pray Heaven we will be in time to save that wretched animal from the consequence of his own vainglory."

Without even changing out of his slippers the Badger set off at a lope, leading the Rat and the Mole and an even bigger retinue of weasels and stoats and ferrets – who, as they scampered follow-my-leader out of the Wild Wood, recruited others to their ranks by answering relatives and neighbours enquiring as to what all the fuss was about with remarks such as, "Mr Toad's grown wings!" and "Come and see the Toad bird!"

The cavalcade reached Toad Hall and headed through the grounds and along the side of the house to the rear lawn that rolled down to the river – and found the area already occupied by as many animals again (for Otter wasn't the only one the heron had told) and all of these, Otter included, staring expectantly up at the roof.

"Thought I'd better cut across here ahead of you chaps to see exactly what was what," said the Otter. "It's true, I'm afraid: Toad has transformed himself into a bird – albeit an insult to the image of any self-respecting bird; he showed himself at a bedroom window a minute or two ago and announced he would shortly appear on the roof to make what he called an historic flight."

The Rat began shouldering his way through the crowd towards the terrace and the French windows opening on to it, shouting: "We must stop the idiot!"

"No use that way!" the Otter advised. "Toad's locked every door and shuttered every window; he must have sensed we'd get wind of what he was up to and try to interfere; I've already tried."

A cry of "There he is!" brought a hush over the gathering on the lawn as a strange apparition began raising itself behind the parapet fifty-foot high on the roof of Toad Hall: a head came into view, a feathered head vaguely resembling that of a Red Indian Chief but not nearly so skilfully neat and splendid; more like a bedraggled old hen; and the beak, a bright orange hooked protuberance, was so long that the tip dipped several inches down the outside of the parapet (even from below it was easy to make out the black elastic holding it to Toad's head). Then Toad lifted a feathered leg to the parapet, hauled up his other leg and stood erect in profile displaying his tail, a cluster of ostrich plumes sticking out from his rear even further than the beak from his face. Puffed with pride, he looked down on his audience (having secretly watched it assemble from behind an upstairs curtain) and deliberately strutted a few steps along the narrow parapet showing off his finery, bringing a gasp from the watchers as he turned waveringly to strut back again.

"Toad!" called the Badger. "What are you doing up there in that ridiculous garb? Come down at once before you fall down."

"Fall down?" Toad called back with a derisive laugh. "There'll be no *falling* down, Badger, I can assure you of that, O no! There will be a *flying* down though; I shall land among you after a trip to that farthest tree-top and, say, half a dozen turns round the lawn just to get the feel of things, then I shall make a flight to the rookery in the Wild Wood and –"

"Toad," called the Badger, "stop braying like a silly ass. Need I remind you it's birds that fly; Toads crawl!"

Toad's feathers seemed to ruffle at this remark and he raised his arms and began flapping them as if about to launch himself into the air without further palaver.

"The days of crawling are over for this Toad!" he yelled, teetering on the parapet recklessly in his anger.

"Wait a minute," said the alarmed Badger, thinking desperately of a way to keep Toad from hurling himself to certain disaster. "I can see that you're a determined fellow and obviously intent on succeeding. But if this is such an important event, such an historic occasion, shouldn't it be recorded for posterity? Shouldn't we, for instance, be taking a photograph so that future generations will be able to share in this glorious moment when the first Toad broke free from his earthly shackles and –"

"By Jove, you're right, Badger!" interrupted Toad, thoroughly delighted. "Why didn't I think of that? I would have done, of course, but I was too busy with preparations for the deed itself. Good old Badger, well done. Have you got a camera?"

"I have, Toad, back at my house. If you wouldn't mind delaying this . . . this historic flight, for a while, I'll send Rat and Mole to collect it and the tripod and the plates and –"

"And the black cloth thing you put over your head, don't forget that, Badger," said Toad, sitting on the parapet and kicking his legs in squirmy delight now that everyone obviously was realising what a brave and clever and important animal he was.

The Badger led the Rat and Mole to the back of the crowd and gave them their instructions.

"You remember how we got into Toad Hall uninvited last time after the weasels and stoats took over while Toad was a guest of Her Majesty because of his motor-car escapade?"

"Twenty years he got," nodded the Mole, "for stealing a motor-car, driving to the public danger and gross impertinence to the rural police!"

"And then he escaped dressed as a washerwoman," said the Rat, "and he came back here and we had to tell him Toad Hall was taken over by the Wild Wooders and you remembered –"

"The secret passage!" said the Mole.

"And we crept along the passage and came up in the butler's pantry," said the Rat, "and we whacked 'em and whacked 'em and routed 'em and restored Toad to his rightful place!"

"Exactly right," said the Badger. "Off you go, the pair of you – up the secret passage, up into the butler's pantry and on up to the roof; but, of course, don't *whack* Toad when you get there: just grab the blighter and hang on to him."

"Hurry up, you two," urged Toad, as the Rat and the Mole set off, "it's glorious flying weather and I'm eager to get started. I could have flown to your place, Badger, and brought the camera here myself to save time – but that would have been cheating I suppose, because then you could only have taken a picture of my *second* flight; no, *there* would be the first, *back* would be the second – my *third* flight. As the world has waited since time began for this day, we may as well keep the record honest and accurate for the sake of a few minutes."

The Badger, itching to get his hands on Toad and shake the conceit out of him and some sound sense into him, asked: "Wouldn't it be wiser to make an experimental flight first from a safer level, say, the lowest branch of a tree, just in case?"

"I've already tried that," said Toad, with a dismissive flick of his paw.

"And you actually flew?"

"Not actually *flew* – well, I *did* actually *fly* but I was down before I knew it – all because I wasn't high enough to start with. From up here it'll be different, you'll see."

"But what makes you *sure* you can fly?"

"Because I worked it out, Badger, that's what. I asked myself, 'Why do birds fly and Toads don't?' The answer came to me like a thunderclap: the only difference between *them* and *us* is that they have feathers and beaks and tails and we haven't. Well, as you can see, it took me no time at all to attend to that detail! How do you like my beak? I'm particularly pleased with it; it's a very valuable beak as a matter of fact. It was the powderhorn carried by my great-great-great Uncle Tobias Toad when he trekked through the interior of Africa before anyone else dared to venture further into that vast, dark continent than the cosy settlements on the coast – *ages* before Livingstone got lost, never mind Stanley finding him. No one believed him when he came back, that was the shameful thing; no one in authority, that is, but the Toads did. O, the exciting tales that have been handed down with this powderhorn! I wish great-great-great Uncle Tobias could be here today to witness my setting the seal on *his* splendid pioneering achievement with my own splendid pioneering achievement wearing his powderhorn as a beak . . . It wasn't orange then, of course; I put a dab of paint on to give it a more

bird-like look . . . Where have those two got to, Badger? Taking their time, aren't they?"

"They'll be here soon," called the Badger, wondering himself why the Rat and the Mole were so long in reaching the roof. "The camera equipment is rather cumbersome and they wouldn't want to risk dropping it and damaging it making undue haste. Tell me, Toad, your big pink tail can't be just an ordinary tail; surely it must have an interesting history . . ."

Toad, the eager monologist, immediately launched into a detailed and highly coloured account of how great-great-great Uncle Tobias had brought the ostrich feathers back from darkest Africa with the powderhorn, and how they had been dyed and made into a boa for his great-great-great Aunt Agatha Toad, who had worn it at all the most splendid of soirees – in Court circles indeed – and had been the envy of all other Society ladies, even the *noblest* of personages, who had never seen anything before so becoming and desirable, resulting in great-great-great Aunt Agatha starting a fashion that was to sweep the whole civilised world.

He was in full spate as the Otter, who had slipped away from the Badger's side, returned and whispered: "Ratty and Mole are hiding round the corner; they've been along the secret tunnel but they can't get up into the house – Toad's bolted the trap-door as well. What are we going to do now?"

The Badger closed his eyes and put a paw to his head.

"O dear," he growled, "what indeed are we going to do?"

He looked up at Toad, who was again strutting along the parapet pointing to his beak and tail in turn and expounding further on his illustrious forebears and the injustice of their unacknowledged achievements; Toad may have been speaking the truth as he knew it, and on the other hand his fertile imagination may have been running away with him; his audience, however, began sitting on the lawn, murmuring discontent at this lengthy prologue to the exciting event they were waiting for.

"Tell Ratty and Mole to go and collect the photographic equipment anyway," the Badger requested Otter. "We might at least have something to remember Toad by . . ."

The Otter made to depart, then took the Badger's arm.

39

"I've an idea," he said. "It *could* work – it had better! I'll see to it after I've despatched Ratty and Mole; keep that blatherskite on the go as long as you can."

As Otter darted away the Badger called: "We know about your splendid beak and magnificent tail, Toad, but your feathered body and arms – er, wings – for the sake of all Toads who are bound to want to emulate you in the future, shouldn't we know something about *them?*"

Toad stopped on the parapet and smoothed down the feathers on his chest.

"O, nothing really remarkable about these, Badger," he said. "Except, of course, the way I personally glued each one to the sheath of silk I'm swathed in underneath. The feathers are from my chickens – Rhode Island Reds, naturally; they lay the best eggs by far, any others are hardly worth the boiling; just two or three feathers plucked from each of them, though *they* weren't very happy about it, I can tell you; but I did give them an extra handful of corn apiece."

The Badger said: "From here, Toad, it seems as if you've moulted in places. Are you sure you've sufficient feathers to keep you in the air? Other birds seem to have many more than you."

A Cockney sparrow, who was a regular though uninvited week-end guest at Toad Hall chirped in, much to the Badger's surprise: "Well, for a start, there's forty farsan' fevvers on a frush's froat alone!"

"Forty farsan' – forty *thousand?*" queried the Badger. "That seems a tremendous number!"

" 'Eard it said many a time," insisted the sparrow. "Gotter be right!"

"You hear that, Toad? This City gentleman says there are forty thousand feathers on a thrush's throat alone: how many have you?"

"O, lots and lots – heaps," replied Toad, covering his throat quickly and turning away. "Plenty."

"Yes, but how many exactly? I feel you'd better count them in the interest of historical accuracy. You may have more than you need; on the other hand, if you can fly with fewer feathers than a thrush it will be an extra feather in your cap, so to speak."

"Twenty-three!" Toad announced without hesitation, puffing up again at his extreme cleverness in managing with so few.

"Only twenty-three at your throat?" asked the Badger.

"Not *all* at my throat – that's right down as far as the bottom of my chest; no need to overdo the feathers side of things, I told myself, it's far more important to *think* your way into the correct frame of mind, to act with the brain of a bird . . . ah, and about time, too: here come those two stout friends with the camera. I'll be ready when you are, Badger."

The Rat and the Mole arrived on the lawn burdened with the photographic equipment and as they began setting it up at the Badger's direction, Otter reappeared and tugged the Badger's arm, whispering urgently.

A look of hope came into the Badger's eyes.

"Good thinking, Otter," he said. "That ought to work – if the timing's right. Now see here: I'll make a signal with my flash powder; I don't need flash powder with the light like this but no one else will know that, least of all Toad. And your friends will then have up to ten seconds to act – impress that upon them: up to ten seconds, no more."

Otter slipped away again as the Badger turned to inspect the camera and tripod positioning.

"You did bring everything?" the Badger asked the Rat. "The flash powder and the tray and –"

"And the black cloth you put over your head, O yes," the Rat assured him. "But Badger, we're surely not going to let Toad go ahead with this madness, are we?"

The Mole shuffled in agitation. "We imagined you'd be thinking of something very clever to dissuade him while we were going through this charade of preparing to take his picture doing what he . . . it mustn't happen! How can we let it happen?"

"I pray that it won't," said the Badger. "Otter has a plan; it's our only hope. If it doesn't work, Toad had better be much more of a bird than we think he is."

The Badger checked the tripod and camera ponderously, realigning one leg of the tripod an inch this way and another leg an inch that way, then lifting the tripod into the air and readjusting all three legs a couple of inches outwards again. He tilted the camera upwards and downwards and manoeuvred it from side to side, and then went through the

41

whole process again with the black cloth over his head, as if finding great difficulty in locating Toad. Various plates were inserted into slots in the camera and removed again, with many a "Tch-tch!" after further inspections under the black cloth.

The fiddlingness of these seemingly endless preparations brought mutterings and loud yawns from the audience, but interest stirred when the Badger stood back and called up: "Toad, do you realise you're standing upside down right now?" He added with an indulgent chuckle: "Not really upside down, of course, only in the camera's eye . . . and we'll soon have you back on your feet – I hope."

Next he poured a huge amount of magnesium powder into his flash pan, much more than would have been needed even in the darkest situation to produce a photograph, and finally stood back again and folded his arms.

"Toad, please pay close attention. I will be taking two photographs of you. The first will be as you stand poised to launch into this historic flight. You will, I assume, have your wings outstretched, you will be raised on your toes . . ."

The Badger added under his breath, as Toad nodded acknowledgement much too urgently: "And no doubt your heart will be in your mouth, my brave but foolish friend."

He went on, proclaiming: "When the flash goes off I will change the photographic plate and recharge the flash pan while counting to ten. As I reach ten, the great moment will be upon us: you will cease to be earthbound. Now – are you quite clear about the timing?"

"Yes, O yes!" replied Toad in a curiously high-pitched voice, stretching out his wings.

"So be it," said the Badger, triggering the flint wheel and firing the flash powder.

A flare of blinding white light seemed to dull the sun, forcing Toad to close his eyes. He stood on the parapet, extended arms atremble and fear surging in him that he might not, after all, have sufficient feathers and that he might not, after all, be sufficiently bird-brained and that he might not, after all, have sufficient will-power to take off when the moment came . . . He heard the Badger counting.

" . . . three . . . four . . . five . . ."

The Badger had just pronounced "Seven" when the air was

*"The camera is ready,"* said the Badger.

filled with the distinctive rhythmic squeak of swans in flight. At "Nine" a pair of them swooped in low over the roof behind Toad. At "Ten", as the Badger triggered his second pan of flash powder, each swan seized Toad by an upper arm with its beak and whisked him in a breathtaking loop high over the lawn, with every head below craned upwards, open-mouthed at the suddenness of Toad's flight and the manner of it.

The swans circled the lawn half a dozen times, streaming the helpless Toad effortlessly between them, his plumage all aflap and aquiver, which *may* have been due to the breeze set up by his passage through the air and not to any uncontrollable tremors in his body; and between the squeaking of the swans' wings, high-pitched "Eeks!" were clearly audible, which *may* have been Toad exulting at his aerial conquest and nothing at all to do with stark terror.

The squeaks and the screeches faded as the swans pointed in the direction of the Wild Wood and carried their passenger all the way to the Rookery there, wheeling around the tall elms a couple of times before heading back to Toad Hall, where they turned in decreasing circles – while maintaining their height – directly over the river.

Otter nudged the Badger: "They are waiting for the next signal."

"The camera's ready," said the Badger. "Ratty and Mole – as fast as you can, go and man a boat; Toad may be no more of a fish than he is a bird."

As the Rat and the Mole ran to Toad's boathouse and pushed out a dinghy, the Badger called up to the sky: "Toad, the real historic moment of truth is almost upon us. Those splendid swans are holding you safely at exactly the same height as your own rooftop; if you could have flown from *there* – as you so publicly proclaimed – you could certainly fly from where you are now; and if you can't fly, well, it's a good thing that the water is deep. When I ignite the flash powder this time, you will be on your own. Prepare yourself!"

Once again the blinding light flared over the lawn, and in that instant the swans released their hold on Toad and were gone in their own snow-white flash.

Toad descended so quickly that the onlookers almost missed the historic occasion.

A streak of orange and pink and a futile flapping of his arms was followed by a splash that drenched those who had rushed to the water's edge in anticipation of what might happen.

Toad took longer to surface from the depths of the river than he had taken to drop into it; his dislodged beak floated up first, and the Mole scooped it out. The Rat, poised in the stern, watched for Toad to emerge in the wake of the froth of air bubbles gushing out from him down below.

Then Toad appeared, gasping desperately for breath, and the Rat got an arm around him, clamping him to the stern.

"Take the oars, Mole," the Rat instructed, "no good trying to get him inboard – he'd have us over. We'll tow him to the bank."

The Badger and Otter were waiting to haul Toad ashore, dragging him on to the lawn where he lay, a pitiful wet heap of matted and crumpled feathers (those that he still possessed, that is, for some had come off during his flight and many more were floating on the river) and he moaned and gurgled as Otter knelt over pumping water out of him by pressing rhythmically on his back.

There was a good deal of sniggering from the onlookers, but it quickly subsided as the Badger turned to them with a sorrowful look and a slow shake of the head.

"This is no time for sneers and jeers," he chided. "Toad is down, so you would kick him, eh?"

The Badger walked among the assembled ranks, who shuffled backwards respectfully as his glance fell upon them.

"Let me tell you," the Badger said with feeling when he was well into their midst, "there is not one of us here today – not one of us other than Toad – with a mind lively enough even to imagine that we may do anything that seems un-natural; I for one would be the first to espouse clinging to the humdrum order of things, never to stray from the tried and well-trodden paths.

"But let me tell you also that our world needs the likes of Toad – adventurous spirits who, if they fail to broaden our horizons at every attempt with their apparently wild notions, then at least illustrate through the discomforts and dangers they may and often do undergo in the process, that our own narrow horizons are all the cosier for their narrowness.

45

"I happen to believe that no Toad, any more than a Badger, was ever meant to fly and never will fly. But as you leave here now to return to the cosiness of your River Bank and Wild Wood paths, having witnessed an adventurous spirit come before a fall, remember this: I also believe that if Toads *could* fly, Mr Toad of Toad Hall *would* have flown this day."

Thereupon the crowd began to disperse silently and thoughtfully, and the Badger returned to where Toad was now being helped to his feet by the Rat and the Mole.

"Now then, Toad," said the Badger, "I take it you have a pocket in that flying suit of yours?"

Toad looked back blankly.

"What I am pursuing," went on the Badger, "is the matter of the key to Toad Hall; after locking us all out so securely, you did think to carry a key with you in order to get in again on coming down to earth?"

"Um, er, O," began Toad, feeling for his waistcoat pocket which, of course, wasn't there, then to his trouser pocket,

which, of course, wasn't there either. Then brightly: "Um –
ah – yes! There's always one in the Secret Place!"

"The Secret Place?"

"Hanging from a string through the letter-box."

"Secret? Why, that's the most *obvious* place – and none of
us thought of looking there; the trouble it would have saved if
someone had."

The Rat retrieved the key and unlocked the door, and the
Badger led the way towards the breakfast room with pur-
poseful step.

"I was about to start my breakfast when I was rudely
interrupted on your behalf, Toad. It's uneatable now, without
doubt, and there's nothing makes me more acidy and grumpy
for days than being deprived of a morning's victuals. Already I
feel the grumpiness coming on – and as you have been the
cause of it you shall provide the balm: three slices of York ham
should be enough – no, better make it four, then I won't need
to bother with lunch; half a dozen of your Rhode Island eggs –
they are large, I hope – a few plump pork sausages, a handful
of fresh mushrooms simmered in butter and a couple of well-
grilled tomatoes.

"The others can place their own orders if they've the
appetite – but I won't have them getting between me and the
coffee: I want a big piping hot pot all to myself – and see that
the milk's heated. O, and don't forget heaps of hot-buttered
toast and coarse-cut marmalade.

"When I've put myself outside of *that* little repast I'll be in
better stomach for putting *you* in your place!"

Toad paused as they passed through the long drawing
room, the hint of a gleam already returning to his eyes.

"Badger," he said, "I *am* an adventurous spirit, aren't I?
The world needs the likes of me, doesn't it?"

"What you are is a reckless fool, Toad," the Badger said
curtly.

"But I heard you telling the others, and I was so *proud* I–"

"That was for their ears, not yours: I was merely trying to
restore some respect for the Toad Hall image. I warn you,
Toad, I'm starting to feel decidedly more acidy."

"But perhaps with a few more feathers," said Toad,
"maybe a thousand or so –"

47

"Not with forty thousand more at your throat alone, you stupid individual!"

" – and with wider wings," went on Toad, "and a running start from an even greater height and –"

"*Stop!*" commanded the Badger in such fury that Toad choked back whatever else he was going to cite as an aid to his conquest of the air. "Take your great-great-great Uncle Tobias's powderhorn from Mole this minute. Now, hold it across your heart with your right hand and say after me: 'I Toad . . .'"

"I Toad,"

" . . . do solemnly swear . . ."

" . . . do solemnly swear . . ."

" . . . that this is a powderhorn and not a beak . . ."

Toad hesitated.

"*SAY* it!" ordered the Badger.

" . . . that this is a powderhorn and not a beak . . ."

" . . . that my tail and feathers are mere frivolous appendages . . ."

" . . . that my tail and feathers are mere frivolous appendages . . ."

" . . .and that henceforth I will never attempt to think like a bird and will remain content to be what I am and always will be – a Toad."

Toad, it seemed to the surprise of the others, repeated the last promise almost happily and then stepped sprightly towards the kitchen, patting his stomach and announcing: "I'm as famished as you are, Badger. Now, how many in all for breakfast?"

\* \* \*

"What does it mean, Ratty," asked the Mole as they paused on their way home to stare down and listen to the river swirling and swishing as it smoothed the boulders under the Iron Bridge, "when someone crosses their fingers?"

"Mmm?" murmured the Rat.

"Why does anyone deliberately cross their fingers?" repeated the Mole.

"O, just superstition," said the Rat. "Hoping for success – trying to ensure against disaster."

"I thought so," said the Mole. "I just wanted to be sure. You see, I can't understand it: what would Toad be hoping for success in now? I could understand him keeping his fingers crossed when he was up there on the roof – but not in his own drawing room where no disaster threatened."

The Rat said: "Toad had his fingers crossed?"

"When he was repeating after the Badger about not doing this and never doing that and so on, he had his right hand with the powderhorn over his heart, and his left hand was behind his back – with his fingers crossed. I don't think he knew I could see."

"O dear," said the Rat, looking back at Toad Hall, "I fear Toady has tricked us all. There's another reason for crossing your fingers and he certainly knows it – we often did it as youngsters in our games: crossed fingers means you are cancelling any oath or promise you may seem to be making."

"So," said the Mole, "Toad doesn't really intend to give up trying to fly!"

"Indeed it looks that way," said the Rat. "But he'll not be making any further attempts today, at least; probably not for a week or so, when he has made himself a bigger and better flying suit."

"O my!" said the Mole. "Now that really upsets me!"

"Don't worry, old chap – as long as we know what's in his mind we can all keep a close eye on him to see he doesn't come to grief."

"I wasn't worrying so much about Toad," said the Mole, looking decidedly downcast, "it was the thought of his poor chickens – all of them standing around half-plucked and shivering."

The Rat laughed loudly at this, mainly because of the Mole's face as he said it, and the Mole's expression quickly changed to one of reproof.

"All right, all right," said the Rat, curbing his laughter, "I know it would be unthinkably unfair if the chickens lost any more feathers for another of Toad's escapades; but don't you see – they can help themselves by helping us: as soon as Toad starts plucking any of them they can send a runner to let us know and we'll soon be there to put a stop to it; I'll make sure they get the message before the day is out. Now come on,

Mole, let's be on our way – there's a lot of work to be done at home; we've not even cleared away the breakfast things yet."

The Rat set off at a smart pace and soon was proclaiming in rhythm with his step:

"Why did the chicken cross the road?
Why, to get away from Toad!
Dreadful Toad!
Grasping Toad!
Stealing all her feathers-o."

He glanced at the Mole. "What do you think of that?"

"Not much," said the Mole. "I mean I wasn't listening properly so I'm not thinking *anything* about it much. What I *was* thinking is: when we get home, is it your turn to wash the dishes and mine to dry – or is it the other way around?"

"Does it matter?" asked the Rat, knowing full well the Mole didn't mind doing the washing part but hated the drying. He leaned backwards and saw quite plainly that the Mole had his left hand behind him – with the fingers crossed. "Supposing you wash and I dry, eh?"

"So be it," said the Mole, uncrossing his fingers and smiling for the first time that day.

# Chariot of Fire

THE MOLE stood at the top of the church tower, engrossed by the view; he hadn't realised things could look so different, depending on where you were when you looked at them.

From down there it had all been wondrous enough, that day he impulsively abandoned his spring cleaning and popped up into the life of the Water Rat: everything then had been new and exciting, a vista of strange scenes inviting undreamt-of meetings and touchings and smellings and tastings.

But from up here, not only distant smoke indicated the Wide World where, the Rat had said, no animal should ever venture: a long, low line of what must be the actual fabric of that awesome place smudged the horizon like a greater and grimmer Wild Wood. With a swift intake of breath the Mole jerked his head behind a tooth of the battlemented parapet at the sudden notion that the Wide World might be looking back.

The Wild Wood, though, clad in its rich High Summer foliage, seemed from this height about as menacing as clusters of soft green cradles that one could drop into and lie gently cushioned. The River, so broad and endless when you were on it, now showed itself no more than a stride wide – but more endless, if that were possible, snaking silently away left and right, the messages of the voices in its reeds and willows failing to reach his ears even as whispers. Cows browsing in a far field were as toy-like as their own byre, sheep on a nearer

51

pasture were (the Mole assessed with singular pleasure) only Mole-size; and try as he might he could detect no evidence of weasels and stoats going about their business – which, of course, they were bound to be doing – but occasional flickers of white in the sunlight just beyond the shadows of hedgerows must surely be the scuts of rabbits hopping to tastier patches.

Even Toad Hall, which had seemed so towering when Toad was poised to fly from it, now appeared merely forepaw high and –

"O my!" uttered the Mole, suddenly reminded of the reason for his being at the top of the tower. He ran his eye out from the churchyard under him, along the lane and over the Iron Bridge all the way to the carriage drive of Toad Hall.

"Well, *is* he or *isn't* he on his way?" the Badger's voice boomed up the steps from the bell ringing chamber. "Can you see him, Mole?"

"Er, not quite, Badger," replied the Mole, quickly flicking his eyes back and forth over the whole length of the route from the Hall to the church, "there's no immediate sign of him but he *could* be close to the hedge or just passing a tree or –"

"Wretched Toad!" exploded the Badger. "I stipulated nine

52

o'clock on the dot – and now it's twenty-past; he'll answer for this when he does appear, mark my words!"

The Mole scrutinised the route more urgently, willing Toad to turn up on it somewhere, until the Badger called again: "Better join us down here, young fellow, no use wasting any more time; may as well get on with teaching you others the ropes, though it'll mean having to go over it all again when Toad shows up. What an irritation!"

The Mole retraced his way down the curving steps for his first lesson in what the Rat had described as campanology but what the Badger had called bluntly, when arranging this occasion: "Bell ringing! That's the answer to Toad's waywardness: keeping a 16cwt Tenor swinging in rhythm will concentrate his mind beautifully – if he doesn't pull his weight the entire neighbourhood will know of it!"

When the Mole had taken his place like the Rat and the Otter alongside one of the five hanging bell ropes, the Badger began: "Your attention, please, gentlemen; we are about to become a band – *if* and *when* our absent friend condescends to make up the number.

"In the next few weeks, for a couple of hours a day – Saturdays and Sundays excluded, of course – I shall be endeavouring to turn you all into fledgling change ringers; a month from now, assuming you apply yourselves to the task with diligence and are imbued with a keen desire to master the art, you may be accomplished enough to attempt your first Grandsire Doubles . . ."

The Badger droned on rather, explaining that a bell was always referred to as *she* and that it was necessary to "ring her up on her wheel by her rope to get her ready for action", and she may be then struck *outward* or *inward* and left *lying still* (foreheads wrinkled at what seemed like double-Dutch). He stressed the importance of *never* looking up to watch your rope coming down again after a pull (everyone immediately looked up the ropes, even though they'd not yet touched them) because that way you'd be bound to miss catching the sally – the coloured tufted section near the rope's end – and ruin the sequence. He spoke of harmonic tones involving the Hum Note and the Fundamental Note and other baffling variations; and to illustrate that bell ringing was all done by numbers he cited arithmetical peaks to be attained, such as a Quarter Peal consisting of 1,260 changes rung without a pause and a Full Peal involving 5,000 or more changes and which took *hours* to complete.

The minds of his pupils, who had been under the impression that bell ringing was merely a matter of much lusty and joyful tugging, began boggling at the thought of all the hard learning they had let themselves in for; only half of one pupil's mind though, that of the Mole, for throughout the Badger's introductory remarks the other half had been dwelling on what he had seen from the top of the tower; so he reacted with alacrity to the Badger's sudden growled aside: "Mole – that Toad; would you just take another look?"

The Mole ascended the curving steps two at a time – and seemed to appear back in the ringing chamber almost as quickly.

"Badger," he called excitedly, "better come and see: something very odd's going on at Toad Hall again!"

They all joined him at the top of the tower, there to stare at a perplexing sight: the Hall seemed to have a huge mushroom sprouting from it, an exotic growth of blue, white and gold stripes that swelled larger as they watched, swaying slowly this way and that as if trying to break away from its root.

The Rat was first to perceive that the strange object wasn't really stemming from Toad Hall but, in fact, emanated from the large paddock immediately beyond.

"I know what *that* is," he said, "Toad's got himself a balloon!"

"A balloon?" said Otter.

"For flying in," said the Rat.

Everyone turned to follow the Badger, already hurtling back down the belfry steps yelling, "Insufferable! Insufferable!"

There was no talk as they padded towards the Hall, each of them preoccupied with Toad's new hazardous intent and how, even if they were in time to influence events on this occasion, they might deflect him from it.

There was no talk either when they drew near the balloon and shuffled to a halt within the orbit of its dazzling spell. It *commanded* a reverential silence.

It was a veritable cathedral of a creation, filling the sky with

54

majestic symmetry, its silken segments of blue, white and gold blazing bright in the sun and bathing them all in a reflected glow as ethereal as though through a stained glass window; a heavenly chariot chafing to be free of the retaining hawsers staked to the paddock, so to arc away on a zephyr bound for its own rainbow's end.

They stood mutely in its magical aura, unable to collect their wits.

At last the Rat forced his eyes from the hypnotic canopy to the wickerwork basket slung below it, following a length of piping looped from the basket to a chimney arrangement over a brazier glowing on the paddock.

He looked back quickly at the sound of a delighted "Ah-ha!" to Toad's face beaming over the edge of the basket.

"Thought it wouldn't take you chaps long to notice what old Toad was up to!" called Toad. "Sorry I didn't see you arrive – just been squaring off the parcels of victuals in here: getting everything ship-shape – air-shape, that is. Like my balloon, do you? Yes, thought you would; was there *anything* more thrillingly splendid? Who's coming with me, eh? Only room for one more, I'm afraid. You, Badger? Ratty?"

A growling and grumping noise came from the Badger, which usually preceded a withering denouncement, but after several "Ers" and a couple of "Umps" followed by a long "Aaaagh," all he came out with rather lamely was: "What about the bell ringing, Toad?"

"Bell ringing?" answered Toad, as if he hadn't heard aright. "Could you possibly have mentioned *bell ringing*, Badger, while I was talking about *ballooning*? Dear o me! Well, pooh to that! Pooh-pooh-pooh-pooh and pooh again to bell ringing! A noisy, clanging waste of time: ruins a chap's Sunday lie-in for one thing. Now – who's coming *ballooning?*"

In the silence that followed the Rat was perturbed to see that the Badger was standing with his eyes lowered, in apparent baffled unease, as if incapable of coping with this assault on the values he knew.

"Toad!" called the Rat, stepping into the breach.

"Ah, Ratty!" Toad acknowledged welcomingly. "I knew *you'd* have the right spirit: climb aboard and we'll be off."

"Off where to?" asked the Rat.

55

Toad parried the question with another, spoken in a tone of condescending patience.

"Am I right in assuming that the wind is from the North?"

"Er, yes – well, what wind there is," said the Rat. "Really just a breeze, but certainly from the North."

"And a wind from the North blows to the South?"

"True."

"Good; that'll take us there. Jump in, Ratty."

"Take us *where*, Toad?" insisted the Rat.

"Why, to that far-off land where my great-great-great Uncle Tobias had such amazing adventures: to Africa, of course!"

"Africa?" said the Rat incredulously. "The only way to get to Africa is by ship – as my cousin the Sea Rat would do. You can't get there in a basket!"

"Can't I though! You'll see – as soon as I release these hawsers my balloon will lift me and my basket up into the sky, and we'll go free as the wind all the way to the Dark Continent; it's full of hot air, you see."

"So are you, Toad!" snapped the Rat, losing patience. "I happen to know about balloons – your hot air will quickly cool, and as you're apparently *not* taking that brazier with you to keep up the supply, you'll be down to earth again in a matter of minutes."

"Very well!" retorted Toad, equally as snappishly, jumping out of the basket and making to untie one of the hawsers. "If no one believes I can do what I intend to do, I'll jolly well do it alone!"

He paused at the sound of another voice asking shyly: "How high will your lovely balloon fly, Toady?"

"Right up there, Mole," replied Toad with a wave at the sky.

"Higher even than the top of the church tower?"

"O much higher; nearly to the sun, I shouldn't wonder."

"I'll come with you then . . .if you'll have me," said the Mole.

The Rat looked in astonishment at his friend as Toad told the Mole enthusiastically: "*Have* you? You're more than welcome, young Mole. It's nice to know someone has faith in me and is blessed with the same visionary outlook. Let us away, you and I – now!"

Blinking with excitement, the Mole started towards the basket but found himself face to face with the Badger, and it was clear as soon as the Badger spoke that he was completely his old self again.

"No you don't, Mole," he said, laying a firm paw on him. "Neither you nor Toad is going anywhere in that infernal contraption; beautiful and enticing it is, I concede, but *devilish* beautiful to my mind; bewitching. I smell danger."

"Please, Badger!" the Mole implored. "I *must* go. It's *wonderful* looking down from there (he pointed back to the church tower), so it must be *heavenly* looking down from right up there (he gazed skywards); don't stop me, *please*, Badger!"

The Otter stepped forward and also laid a paw on the Mole, saying: "No, my friend, I too sense danger. For one thing (the Otter was now addressing Toad) just supposing you did manage to get to Africa, how, might I ask, would you propose getting home again?"

"Mercy me, Otter," retorted Toad, "what an unexpected question from one whose intelligence I've always held in such high esteem! The answer's obvious: if a wind from the North carries us *there*, a wind from the South will carry us back! You follow?"

"O yes," said Otter, "and a wind from the East would carry you West and a wind from the West would blow you East – and for all you know they may be the only winds they have in Africa apart from the North Wind, *if* the North wind ever reaches Africa, that is. Not even *you* can *order* the wind, Toad."

Toad hesitated, then deliberately flicked more loops of the first hawser from its stake.

"Naturally I thought of that," he said, his eyes rolling as he thought about it for the first time, "and naturally I have the logical answer: it may indeed be true that there is no South wind in Africa, but having arrived on the North wind we'll just spend a day or two exploring and adventuring then . . . then we'll rise again on that same North wind and it will blow us round the world right back here. The world *is* round, you know – or haven't you heard?"

At this the Badger and Otter took an even firmer hold on the Mole, who turned despairingly to the Rat; and the Rat saw in his friend's face something of the same burning urge to seek new horizons which he himself had been gripped by after his wayside encounter with the salty Sea Rat. There was in the Mole's eyes a plea for help in taking this chance to rise even further from his lowly upbringing than the heights he had achieved by his baptism of sunlight and warmth and the endowment of good experiences that resulted from his discovery of the River Bank. The Rat felt the transmitted yearning; it touched his heart, stirring a desire buried there that had gone unfulfilled through the Mole's well-intentioned and sensible intervention but which, nevertheless, still induced wistful thoughts of what might have been each Autumn when the swallows were preparing to turn their backs on the Winter and follow the sun.

The Rat examined the balloon again, then lifted the Badger's paw from the Mole and held it in his own, drawing him away out of earshot of the others.

"Let them go, Badger," he urged.

"What, Ratty?" replied the Badger. "You of all creatures even entertaining such a nonsensical notion? Upon my word! This escapade is even more hare-brained than Toad's bird-brained performance – and you would let Mole be a part of it! Africa, indeed!"

The Rat pointed to the top of the balloon: where it had been rounded and firm only a few minutes ago, it was now flattening and sagging.

"Africa was a preposterous goal," he said, "and I'd say the hedge at the far end of the paddock was now equally as unattainable. I'd be surprised if they even got off the ground."

The Badger looked unconvinced, so the Rat confided: "I've read about these things: if Toad had filled his balloon with gas we'd have something to worry about; but not when it's only hot air, cooling off by the second. If we let Mole go, he *and* Toad will get something out of their systems. I'm sure there's little danger."

Casting a suspicious eye at the balloon, then regarding the Mole's pining countenance, the Badger told the Rat with a shrug of resignation: "Well, if you have a knowledge of these matters that I have not, I'll not stand in Mole's way – though against my better judgement. Be it on your head if aught befalls him."

The Badger turned away and the Rat, not without a surge of misgiving at the responsibility he had taken upon himself, stepped towards the balloon, beckoning the Mole to approach.

"Toad," he said, "Mole *is* to come with you and I just hope you know what you're doing because if anything should go wrong I'd –"

"Of *course* I know what I'm doing, Ratty," interrupted Toad. "I've read nearly a *whole* book on ballooning, I'm probably one of the world's greatest experts on the subject – climb in, Mole, we've wasted enough time."

The Rat gave the Mole a leg up to the basket, where that excited animal searched around inside for foot room among the supply of food Toad had provided for the journey: two whole boiled hams and six roasted chickens in greaseproof paper, a side of bacon, tins of sardines by the dozen, and a mound of apples and oranges cornered by a churn of milk and two cartons of tinned corned beef.

"Unlash the hot air supply pipe, Mr Mole!" ordered Toad, as if he were Captain Bligh addressing Mr Christian. And then: "Ratty, release that other hawser when I'm aboard, there's a good chap, and we'll be gone."

The Rat took the turns off the stake, pausing at the last. "All set?" he asked.

"Thank you, Ratty," the Mole called from his perch on the cases of corned beef. "Thank you for being so understanding. I'll . . . I'll miss you while I'm in Africa."

"Good luck, my friend," answered the Rat, unflicking the final turn. "Come home safely – and soon."

He waved back as Toad and the Mole waved goodbye. The Otter and even the Badger waved.

The balloon and the basket, free of all earthly ties, stayed firmly on the ground.

After several seconds Toad leaned from the basket, pulled a cord and released sand from one of eight bags hanging two to a side.

The balloon remained earthbound.

He moved round the basket, carrying out the same

procedure and murmuring "That should do it" each time, until all the bags had been emptied – and nothing changed excepting that the basket was now surrounded by eight miniature sandhills.

"I think you may be overloaded," pointed out the Rat.

"Of course we are!" said Toad irritably. "I budgeted on travelling alone. Throw out a case of corned beef, Mr Mole, we'll just have to tighten our belts."

The Mole struggled to do as bidden, but this achieved, the basket stayed rooted to the paddock.

"And another, Mr Mole," commanded Toad, seizing a whole ham himself and flinging it through the air.

The side of bacon came next, followed by three chickens and tin after tin of sardines.

Finally Toad yelled in desperation: "The milk churn! We'll just have to go thirsty – out with it!"

The Mole heaved at the bottom of the heavy churn as Toad hauled it up by its handles. In his enthusiasm, the Mole heaved again mightily just as Toad was balancing it on the edge of the basket, preparatory to lowering it over. Taken by surprise, Toad was still holding on to the handles as the churn toppled to the paddock, tugging him with it.

Dazed and winded, he lay watching the balloon raise the basket a couple of feet in the air and carry it and the Mole away with gathering speed.

"My balloon! Come back, Mole!" gasped Toad, as the Mole gesticulated helplessly at his own predicament.

The Rat, who had been as surprised as anyone by this dramatic development, ran and stooped and ran and stooped again, trying to seize the end of a trailing hawser to arrest the balloon's momentum. He had covered a third of the paddock, attempting and failing to manage this, when a roaring and spluttering sound like that of a malfunctioning motor car assailed his ears.

He stopped in his tracks and gawped as he caught sight of a weird creation like a huge skeletal dragonfly winging in low, directly at right angles to the path of the balloon.

The nose of the frightening contraption appeared to bite the top of the canopy, which split as if slashed and collapsed rapidly in deflated disarray on the grass, dragging the basket

*"My balloon! Come back, Mole!" gasped Toad.*

on to its side and rolling the Mole out on a cascade of apples and oranges.

"Are you all right?" the Rat asked anxiously as he caught up and helped the Mole to his feet. "What a frightening experience!"

"Just a bruise or two," said the Mole, rubbing his shins, "nothing broken. What happened?"

"*That* happened," said the Rat, indicating the strange creation now standing quietly a couple of hundred yards to their left.

"What is it?" asked the Mole in a frightened whisper.

"The manner of its arrival tells me it must be what I've read about in the papers but never believed in and certainly never expected to see," said the Rat. "It must be a flying machine."

As they watched, a man who had been sitting in or on the machine stepped down from it. He was attired in riding breeches and boots and a Norfolk jacket, with a muffler wound around his neck and hanging down front and back, a peaked cap which he wore back to front and a big pair of goggles.

He removed the goggles and strode towards the balloon, reaching it as the same moment as the Badger and Otter; but the Rat noticed that Toad wasn't joining them: he was moving slowly and open-mouthed in the direction of the flying machine.

"I say," began the stranger, addressing the Rat, "I'm awfully sorry about your balloon. Bit of bad luck my running out of petrol like that just when you were launching her – I'd no option, d'you see, had to put down where I could. I'll pay for the damage, of course."

The Rat nodded towards Toad, who was now circling the flying machine, stepping forward and touching a part of it, drawing back and clasping his head in both hands, moving round and bending double and looking underneath and rushing forward and seemingly stroking it.

"It's not my balloon, sir," said the Rat, "it's his. But I'm afraid Mr Toad is already showing a depressing lack of interest in its well-being."

Toad seemed in a trance when they approached. His mouth kept on opening and shutting and a whirring noise came from his throat. When the man spoke, Toad turned worshipping eyes upon him as if he were some kind of god.

"I was just apologising to your friends for the mishap to your balloon," said the man. "I was unable to prevent colliding with it, I'm afraid, because my flying machine had used up the fuel supply. My fault entirely, of course . . ."

"Flying machine," mouthed Toad. "*Flying* machine! *Machine* for flying in! *Flying machine!*"

"I can see you're interested," said the man. "Perhaps you would allow me the honour of showing you over it. It's a French design, you'll appreciate – they're by far the best at it to date – I built it to the specification of one of their leading chaps, name of Bleriot. He's *very* keen but I'm even keener: I aim to be the first aviator to fly right across the English Channel."

He pointed to the engine, which "drives this, the airscrew, which propels the machine through the air and which,

incidentally was what clipped your balloon, sir, as I was coming in to land – and my sincere apologies again for that mishap, but you will understand the difficulty I was in."

"O, please don't give that silly balloon another thought, sir," insisted Toad, "it should never have been in your way! I pray heaven it hasn't damaged your wonderful machine, the very thought appals me. Take lunch with me, sir, and you'll find no more attentive ears waiting upon every word of your glorious exploits and the how and the why and the wherefore of it all. Spare no detail, sir, I implore you . . ."

Toad, oblivious to everything but the machine and its owner, walked off with him, leaving his friends standing uncertainly. Words like "wings" and "rudder" and "elevators" and "pitching" and "yawing" spoken enthusiastically by the aviator and accompanied by graphic hand movements – repeated and imitated even more enthusiastically by Toad – wafted back to them. Toad ushered the aviator through the portal of the Hall, and the door closed firmly behind them.

The Badger sighed deeply. "Same old Toad," he said, "off with the old, and on with the new."

He nodded at the crumpled canopy.

"*That* is undoubtedly *that*; we'll have no more ballooning capers to worry about. But *this* (he indicated the flying machine) is something that *someone* will have to worry about and I tell you all – that someone is not going to be me. I'm out of my depth in these matters, as I admitted to Ratty here. Call it reactionary if you wish – nothing will change my view that Toad's aerial aspirations are an unnecessary and reckless indulgence. But now he has a new friend – who gets invited to lunch when his old friends don't – well qualified, it would seem, to take him under his . . . er, wing, so to speak. So *this* old friend will allow the pair of them to get on with it, and good luck to them.

"In the meantime, let us not waste the victuals that Toad has apparently discarded along with those who always had his interest at heart. Take a ham and a couple of chickens, Otter, and make sure that lad of yours, little Portly, has a good tuck-in. You too, Rat and Mole – and fill your pockets with fruit. I myself will settle for a tin of corned beef, to which I'm very partial when it's thin-sliced and coldly-crumbly, and a tin or two of sardines – as long as they're in olive oil and not that ghastly tomato sauce."

* * *

The Rat and the Mole sauntered home, the one with a ham on his shoulder, the other with a roast chicken under either arm, and both of them munching apples. The Mole had the suggestion of a swagger in his walk, which vaguely irritated the Rat, though he forebore mentioning it.

"Pity about my not actually getting to Africa, wasn't it, Ratty?" observed the Mole.

The Rat looked sideways at his companion.

"Not actually getting to Africa? Why, you didn't actually get *anywhere*, never mind Africa!"

"O come now, Ratty, I did at least set off to go there, which is more than anyone else I know has ever done. We balloon-ists are –"

"*We* balloonists?" exploded the Rat, throwing an apple core at the Mole's head and missing by a mile. "You're getting to be as bad as Toad! Might I remind you, *Mister* Mole, that but for my intervention you would never have been allowed to get into that basket, and I spoke up only because I knew you couldn't have gone far even if the flying machine hadn't appeared. You can't call that *ballooning*!"

"O, what would you call it, then?"

The Rat didn't speak immediately and when he did it was not a reply to the Mole's question.

"Mole," he said, "you have the distressing habit of sometimes talking with your mouth full – especially when eating apples."

"Huffy-huffy!" the Mole chided. "Just because *you've* never been ballooning!" Then he grinned. "I'm pulling your leg, Ratty; I concede that I just got carried away . . . and to tell you the truth I didn't much care for the experience. My heart was in my mouth. The top of the church tower is high enough for me from now on. Do you suppose Toad will be with us tomorrow for the bell ringing?"

The Rat was quite definite. "Not Toad, not tomorrow! Not

65

the day after tomorrow or the day after that, not even next week, I'll warrant, while that flying machine comes between him and his wits."

"Yes, you're right, of course," said the Mole. "Well now, if we couldn't get on with the learning today without Toad, there'd be no point in turning up tomorrow without him, would there?"

"No point at all!" said the Rat, suddenly putting a spring into his step. "No point at all, by Jove! My goodness, how wise you're becoming, Mole; there'll be no need to go bell ringing for *ages* – for the whole idea was to involve Toad . . . I wonder what we shall do to fill in the time, you and I?"

The Rat pulled two apples from his pocket and marched on, juggling them one-handed in the air, expertly and happily, bursting into song with –

"A boat leaves a fizzy fresh wake,
Whichever direction you take.
With hisses and bubbles
It irons out troubles,
Though timbers may shiver and shake.
O, give me a boat, any old boat,
Narrow or broad at the beam . . ."

The Mole bit into yet another apple and jinked along in the Rat's wake.

"I don't need three guesses as to how we'll fill in the time," he said with his mouth full, but really only to himself.

# Adventures of an Aviator

IT WAS late afternoon, and the Rat was dabbing paint on scuffed patches of the boat's washstrake as he digested a more than ample intake of Toad's chicken and ham ballooning rations – which had gone down very agreeably with plenty of chopped chives on the salad – while the Mole was thinking in terms of putting the kettle on for tea, when the roar of an engine filled the air.

They raised their eyes at the approach of the mechanical dragonfly and watched it veer left and right and right and left and nose up and down, and seemingly, at one stage, travel sideways as it passed overhead.

"He's off once more," said the Mole, waving at the hunched figure protruding from the machine in goggles and back-to-front cap, with his scarf streaming in the airflow.

"Better him than me," said the Rat. "Doesn't seem to have much control, does he? Wonder where he'll end up next?"

The sound of the machine grew fainter as it departed erratically in the direction of the Wide World, and then silence returned – or at least nothing could be heard but the swishings and rustlings and babblings and birdsong that passed for silence along the River Bank.

The Mole put the kettle on and had just returned with a pot of tea and a plate of potted meat sandwiches to share with the Rat sitting in the boat, when the sound of another mechanical contraption disturbed the tranquil scene. Toad's motor car

67

drew up – which in itself was surprising: Toad had left it languishing unloved and uncared for in a stable long before the onset of his flying mania. More surprising was that it was not Toad in the driving seat, but the aviator who had descended on Toad Hall out of the blue that morning; and it was obvious, as he jumped from the motor car, that he was extremely agitated.

"Hello," the Rat greeted him, "has something gone amiss again? We saw you passing overhead a short while ago and we waved, but you were very intent on the task in hand and –"

"That wasn't me!" shouted the aviator. "That was your friend Toad – he's absconded with my machine!"

The Rat and the Mole looked at one another in disbelief.

"Are you saying it was Toad we saw above us?" asked the Rat.

"I am indeed!" stormed the aviator. "Such perfidy! Me of all people allowing myself to be tricked by a Toad!"

"He tricked you?" asked the Mole.

"Of course he did! Charmed me into a false sense of comradeship, then stabbed me in the back. Splendid lunch he laid on, non-stop questions I was glad to answer about *exactly* how my machine worked, *what* one did to make it go up and

*what* one did to make it turn and *what* one did to make it come down. I told him happily, chapter and verse – and I can still hear his flattering accompaniment to my explanations, such as 'How clever of you!' and 'How wonderful!' and 'How marvellous!' Positively oozed charm and hospitality, he did. Then it was, 'I've cans and cans of spare fuel in my stable that I'll never use, let us proceed to replenish your machine without delay and get you on your way again.' We filled the fuel tank to the brim, then it was, 'Just let me don your goggles and cap and scarf' and 'Just let me sit where you sit in the machine so I may have an inkling of what it's like to be really flying.' And I allowed him to. Then it was, '*This* is the control stick that points the nose up if I pull it back and down if I push it forward, isn't it? And we bank left if I push it left, and right if I push it right, yes? And these pedals work the rudder on the tail, which turns the machine in the direction we wish to go?'

"Never before had anyone shown quite such a keen interest, and I never suspected what was in the mind of that devious animal even when he implored, 'Please, please swing the airscrew and start the engine so that this poor earthling may feel the power that takes you soaring to the realm of the gods!'

"Like a fool I did – after opening the throttle only a fraction and warning him not to touch it – and the next thing I know he's roaring across the paddock and away . . ."

The man added bitterly: "All those months I toiled assembling my machine, all those hours I spent modifying it and nursing and coaxing it to travel longer and higher and faster, all to one end – as I told him – to make my mark on history. So many others are on the verge of attempting the Channel – someone's bound to succeed soon – and now there's no chance that it will be me, with my machine in the hands of that criminal!"

The Rat said: "I can understand your distress, sir, and I sympathise – but I worry for Toad: with no experience of flying machines, surely he must be in grave danger?"

"He certainly is!" said the man. "It was more by good luck than good management that he actually got into the air, barely scraping clear of the paddock hedge. How he'll get down again – or where – I shudder to think. I don't expect to see my machine again in one piece."

"O my, where should we start looking?" asked the Mole.

"It's a job for the police: I'm driving Toad's motor car back to town now to alert them. He could descend anywhere within a radius of about twenty miles when his fuel runs out – but even before that, this storm rolling in from the West will probably knock him down: just look at those black clouds."

Even as he spoke there was a menacing rumble of approaching thunder and almost immediately the air was disturbed by a fresh wind, which swished the trailing willow branches and sang among them. The song, it seemed to the Mole, had the mournful notes of a lament.

\* \* \*

Every able bodied animal on the River Bank and in the Wild Wood turned out to search for Toad, which may seem surprising in view of his facility for raising the hackles of so many of them so frequently with his insufferable conceit and arrogant air of superiority. It might be thought some would even revel at his misfortune, or shrug off the news saying: "Toad got himself into this predicament – so let him get himself out of it if he's as clever as he professes to be."

But no one adopted either attitude, for in times of trouble, animal nature being what it is, old scores are submerged (to resurface later when all's well again, to be sure) and only pleasanter memories dwelt upon, and Toad, for all his shortcomings, had engendered a fair share of these.

Weasels and stoats, normally given to finding only a grudging good word for this landed gent up at Toad Hall, were in the forefront of the brigade that set forth at first light after the night of storm to find and bring succour to him, now that he was just another fellow creature in distress.

The Rat and the Mole encountered many a Wild Wooder as they trekked mile after mile equipped with a tent, packs of sandwiches and flasks of tea, and a first aid kit containing bandages, ointment, iodine and splints for supporting broken limbs.

"I've looked *that* way," a weasel or stoat popping up in their path would say, "and there's no sign of him *there* so now I'm going *this* way."

Rabbits were out in hundreds, young and old, bounding from field to field and stopping only briefly to nibble a dandelion leaf or two to keep up their energy; and the one who had distinguished himself at the cricket match after Toad's coaching gratefully accepted tea and sandwiches and shelter for the night, when the Rat and the Mole wearily pitched tent a long way from their own home and his at the end of the first day's fruitless reconnaissance.

Otter first swam tirelessly downstream to a point where the River had long ceased to be a familiar world even to him, pausing every few hundred yards to enquire news of Toad or the flying machine from local inhabitants and obtaining, without any urging, their whole-hearted co-operation in joining the search themselves. Then he swam all the way back upstream against the strengthening flow to where the River divided into two rivulets, and spread the word at those crossroads before returning dispirited to the bosom of his family, but determined to go even farther afield on the morrow.

The Badger, on learning of Toad's disappearance, had wasted not a second, striding off as the storm was howling its

worst, zig-zagging methodically across acre after acre in the drenching rain and fearsome thunder and lightning before being prevailed upon to settle for a few hours, albeit restlessly, at the home of a cousin he hadn't seen for years.

The cousin had neither sight nor sound of Toad to report, but promised a full turn out of all *his* neighbours in the morning. When he went to rouse the Badger to join those other good fellows just before dawn, the Badger was already on his way again, nosing through the dark.

But one by one, and in downcast groups, the seekers returned to the Wild Wood and the River Bank after days and nights away, their faces expressive of failure.

And the rooks, it was, who set what seemed like a seal of finality on the fate of Toad.

"We have looked far and wide," reported their leader, "farther and wider and faster than anyone could manage on foot, and nowhere is there a trace of him or his machine. It may be, of course, he ventured where we would hesitate to spread wings, into the very heart of the Wide World."

The Badger, his face drawn and tired with exertion and anxiety, groaned at this.

"Heaven help that poor animal," he said, taking out a hanky and blowing his nose loudly, "if he ended up *there*."

\* \* \*

The storm proved to be no more than a violent hiccup in an otherwise perfect summer, which quickly caught its breath and resumed its pacific pace of early sunrises that made staying in bed a second longer an ordeal, stretched-out balmy days to be savoured coolly in shady nooks, and late sunsets it seemed a sin to drag your eyes from.

Such summers came around not so frequently that anyone could afford to waste a moment of pleasurable outdoor indulgence, especially – as is usually the case – old heads were nodding wisely and forecasting a severe winter ahead, having read *this* sign or *that* sign and quoting the infallibility of their grandfathers in such matters.

But these particular halcyon days drifted by unsung along the River Bank.

Otter seldom showed himself in the water and even then,

not as if he were enjoying himself but only out of a need to be there from time to time; the Badger seemed to have hibernated early; the Rat went for solitary, pensive rows in the boat, finding backwaters in which to lie gloomily on his oars, leaving the Mole pouring interminably over the page of a book that was still unturned when he came back.

Hearts and minds were clouded despite the clear blue skies, for two weeks had gone by and still there was no word of Toad.

The sixteenth day dawned equally as brightly, if not quite so early, but it wasn't the sun streaming in through the window that awakened the Rat.

It was the sound of the church bells, only one of them at first, but then two and haphazardly three, being struck in no recognisable pattern except *dongingly*.

The Rat glanced up, still musing sleepily over the cause of the cacophony, as the Mole came into his bedroom with a wide-eyed, questioning look.

"Well, it's not you and it's not me," said the Rat, jumping out of bed. "It couldn't be Otter, could it?"

"Or Badger, summoning us for some reason?" suggested the Mole.

They dressed hurriedly, pulling on jackets and trousers over their pyjamas, and set off at a gallop for the church. Half way there, each of the questions they had posed about the possible identity of the bell ringer was answered: the Badger and Otter appeared from different directions. All four took in the baffled expression on one another's faces as the clanging continued, then they strode on without further ado to the church, where the Otter led the way up to the bell ringing chamber.

"Well I never!" he exclaimed on the chamber's threshold, venting the feelings of them all as they jostled in behind him and saw what he saw.

Toad was the bell ringer. He leapt from rope to rope, tugging on them uninhibited by any awareness of his audience.

"Toad, it's *you!*" shouted the Badger in joy and relief, whereupon Toad stopped in mid-leap, turned and beamed at them.

"Of course it's me!" he said, walking over open-armed. "I knew the bells would bring you; 'Ring out, wild bells, to the wild sky,' I told myself, 'and your dearest friends will soon be on hand to be first to hear of your triumph!' You'll never guess, not even if I give you from now till doomsday, where I've been or what I've done . . ."

It was a thinner Toad than the one they had last seen, and a tired-looking one despite the gleam in his eye.

"You got down safely, then," said the Rat.

"Got down, yes," replied Toad with a laugh, "not safely exactly, but down certainly. I'm perfectly all right I assure you – let me tell you about —"

"*You're* all right, are you?" the Badger said abruptly. "How very nice! Well let *me* tell *you*, Toad, that *we* are *not* all right! Have you given a thought to what we've been going through these last two weeks? Have you the slightest appreciation of what the entire community has suffered because of your . . .

74

your criminal deceit and treachery? *You're* all right, are you! Toad the selfish! Toad the insensitive! Toad the liar! Toad the thief! *You're* all right, are you, by Heaven? And is the flying machine you stole all right also, eh?"

"Not stole, Badger!" said Toad, his face now crimson. "Merely borrowed, I assure you. I know where it is – at least I know where it was – and I'm making immediate arrangements as soon as I can lay hands on my cheque book to buy that poor gentleman another one."

"Another one?" said Otter. "Where, then, is the other one?"

"Please listen and I'll explain," said Toad. "I'm truly sorry for any distress I may have caused anybody – but when you hear what happened you are going to be so proud of me and so glad I did what I did; and Badger will withdraw those hurtful things he just said about me."

Toad raised the sally of a bell rope and examined it. Then he swung it away so that the rope went circling around him as he declaimed theatrically: "I wish to announce that I have become the first aviator to fly across the Channel!"

"O dear, O lor'," said the Badger after a deep intake of breath, lowering himself to the floor and resting his head on his arms over raised knees. Otter sat down next to him, and the Rat sat down next to *him*, leaving the Mole and Toad the only ones standing.

The Mole, thinking he would rather be sitting down with the others, but sensing he had left the move too long to be anything less than a *personal* slighting of Toad felt it necessary to cover his exposure with the stammering observation: "Er . . . we saw you passing overhead, Toad – that is, Ratty and I saw you . . . and we both were of the opinion that – when we were told it was you, of course, and *not* the aviator man – you didn't seem very much at home, as it were, in the flying machine, and —"

"Let him get on with it, Mole," growled the Badger. "Sit down and let Toad tell his *alleged* account of things; we haven't all morning to spare for this claptrap."

"I'm *not* talking claptrap!" protested Toad. "It's true I wasn't completely master of the machine when Mole saw me – but that was only at the very beginning. In no time at all I became a part of it; soon I was soaring and banking and pitching and yawing at will . . . I was magnificent! Never had I felt so much in my element as I did up there, with the world belittled below and the endless sky all around. I was like an eagle! Believe me, my dear friends, you haven't lived until you have lived as I have, feeling air like champagne tingling your cheeks with its rushing sparkle and intoxicating you with every blessed bubbling breathful. Onwards I flew, straight as a die, with no hedges in my path, no gates to open, no corners to turn, no level crossing to keep me champing at the bit, no irritating policeman holding his hand up, no —"

"Get on with it!" growled the Badger.

"Then the sky darkened," said Toad, shivering at the memory (and the listeners knew that this part of his story, at least, was true) "and a wind suddenly seized the machine and hurled it even further aloft. One moment it was standing on its nose, the next on its tail, the next on its side . . . I was being tossed and blown like a dried leaf. Then thunder burst upon me from every side, cracking like shellfire and shaking the machine until I was sure it was falling apart. The darkness became so intense and rain lashed my face so blindingly that I could no longer see the land below, even when the machine was on its nose, except when lightning flashed like your camera, Badger, illuminating the dire situation in which I now found myself. The wind howled so loudly and the thunder thundered so deafeningly that I was no longer aware of whether my engine was functioning or not, but on and on I went, totally at the whim of the storm. Twinkles of luminosity appeared below me and in the fleeting flare of the lightning, I saw, to my astonishment, vessels battling their way through foam-flecked water. I admit to a certain apprehension at this stage. 'You're a lost soul, Toad,' I told myself over and over again.

"How long the storm held me in its grasp I do not know, but suddenly I felt the machine's momentum arrested as if it had been snatched from the air. I heard a splintering and snapping and saw stars – my head must have banged against something hard which rendered me unconscious, for the next I knew the storm had abated and I was looking out upon a beautiful sun-dappled countryside. I thought at first I was

*The sky darkened and a wind suddenly seized the machine.*

back here, at home, and had awakened from a dream that had turned into a nightmare. Then I saw that I was not on the ground: I was still sitting in the flying machine and *it* was crumpled about me – in the top of a tree! It was an apple tree, and I picked an apple hanging near my head and munched into it; it wasn't really ripe.

"Voices came to me from below. I observed through the leaves two figures – the one in peasant garb, the other in a uniform. 'Hello!' I called. 'Kindly assist me down from here, you chaps – I'm starving of hunger!' A ladder was fetched and propped against the tree, and the uniformed one came up it and helped me to descend. 'Thank you, my good fellow,' I told him as I regained terra firma once more, offering my hand – whereupon he seized my wrist, twisted me backwards and held me in a half-Nelson. 'What's this?' I demanded, outraged.

"The peasant, a particularly surly representative of his class, was gesticulating in apparent anger, pointing to the apples lying around which had been shaken from the tree by my arrival in it and talking gibberish that I couldn't begin to understand; some dialect different from that of the peasants in *our* part, I assumed. Then the uniformed chap spoke – just a few words, right alongside my ear – and one of his words was *'grenouille'* and another *'boucherie'*."

Toad paled and ran his paws down his thighs as far as his knees, as if reassuring himself they were still there.

He continued with a note of hysteria in his voice: "Do you realise he was speaking French? I had landed in France – and it was as if I had fallen into the hands of cannibals! This individual was referring to *me* as a frog! And in the same breath he was talking about the butcher's shop!

"A chap in the French class at school had once called me 'an ugly *grenouille*', and I punched the blighter's head later when I'd looked up its meaning in the dictionary.

"Now I shouted at the peasant and the fellow pinioning me, 'I am *not* a frog! I am Mr Toad of Toad Hall, a very respected landowner in England! And a pioneer aviator!'

"Thereupon the uniformed one began propelling me away – I won't say *frogmarched* me – and I searched my mind desperately for some means of communicating with him in his

78

own lingo. '*Combien des saucissons y-a-t'il dans la boucherie?*' I demanded."

Toad paused, with a wild look of triumph in his darting eyes. The effect on his audience was complete bafflement.

"Why did you ask how many sausages there were at the butchers?" said the Rat.

"Because," Toad informed him, "it was the only French phrase I could remember, apart from the answer. As a matter of fact I was top of the class at asking that question – the master congratulated me on my beautiful accent so I concentrated on saying it absolutely perfectly, though I forgot everything else he taught me.

"The peasant looked at me in some amazement after I spoke; then he had the gall to shrug and say, '*A la boucherie!*' and the uniformed one jerked me forward.

" '*Un moment!*' I insisted – I think 'one' is 'un' – in fact I'm sure of it, because *vingt-et-un* is twenty-one; '*Il y a vingt-et-un saucissons dans la boucherie!*' "

The rat asked: "How did you know there were twenty-one sausages at the butcher's?"

"I didn't," replied Toad. "That's what it said in my school textbook. But it made *them* stop and think, I can tell you! The uniformed one even released my wrist while they discussed the matter, arms waving like windmills, and I seized my chance and fled for my life into the trees. But it was no use; they chased and caught me again and dragged me back and forced me to climb the apple tree with a hammer, smash the flying machine to smithereens and throw the pieces down. It took me nearly all day; a heartbreaking task – but worse was to come. When I'd stacked the bits of the machine in a neat pile I was taken at the point of a pitchfork to an outbuilding of the peasant's farmhouse and chained up in it like a dog for the night. He brought me my supper – a bowl of water, a piece of dry bread and a sausage! Phew, that sausage reeked, it stank of disgusting garlic! Ugh! Nothing turns my stomach more. So though I was dying from lack of food I ate only the bread and drank the water, pushing the sausage as far away from me as possible.

"In the morning I was freed from my chain – to milk three cows and then clean out pigsties which couldn't have been cleaned out since Napoleon's time, while the peasant stood over me with his pitchfork. I had to milk the cows again before being chained up once more – and given another sausage!

"I stormed and raved trying to make the wretch understand I couldn't bear to touch his loathsome provender, but he merely shrugged and slammed the out-house door on me. I was now so weak through toiling without anything inside me but a crust of bread that I steeled myself, held my breath and gulped down both sausages as fast as I could.

"The next night I was given another sausage for my hours of back-breaking labour, *and* on the next – and when I was tackling the seventh of those revolting creations the terrible truth dawned on me: *I had been sentenced to twenty-one sausages with hard labour!*"

Toad displayed the palms of his paws to his audience. They were covered in blisters.

"Something had to be done – and quickly," he said chokingly, "if I was ever to see my beloved homeland again and those dearest to me were to learn of my triumph and my ordeal."

"So?" said the Badger.

"My chance came in the hayfield," went on Toad. "I was scything away – heaven knows how long it would have taken me to cut *that* lot on my own – while the peasant stood idly by as usual. I noticed he'd brought two pitchforks this day, but I knew by now that one would be for me to wield while he leant on the other!

"Presently he sat down, while I continued scything and sweating in the sun. Soon afterwards he was lying down – and then I heard him snore. I crept towards him with the scythe . . ."

"Toad, you didn't *scythe* him, did you?" said a tremulous voice. It was that of the Mole.

"No, no!" said Toad. "Nothing like that crossed my mind. What I did, I took up one pitchfork . . . and slowly and carefully pressed the two prongs their full depth into the soil on either side of his recumbent left arm, pinioning that arm in a metal grasp. Then I took the other pitchfork and did the same with his right arm – and *I* was the master now! I didn't wait to let him know that; I slung his luncheon satchel over my shoulder – he'd *never* shared anything with me at midday – and went as fast as my legs would take me through the uncut hay and deep into the adjoining forest in a truly heroic burst to freedom! I knew I had more than a head start: even when the peasant awoke and realised what had happened, he would have great difficulty in prising the pitchforks from the ground. I ran for the rest of the day and hid myself exhausted as night fell in a briar patch – look, you can see the scratches on my arms still – and in the darkness I opened the peasant's satchel and felt what proved to be a bottle of rough but palatable wine, a loaf of bread, a dozen or so sourish olives and three – I could tell by their odour even before I fingered them – three of those sausages. I wolfed down the bread and the olives; like manna from Heaven, it was, and swilled the wine; and slept for who knows how long from my exertions.

"Lucky I saved the sausages, though; they were all that would sustain me for the next day and a night in that far off land, and there would be only berries and raw turnip and the

81

like borrowed from fields on the way during the hours and hours it took me to walk back here after setting foot in England's green and pleasant land again."

Toad closed his eyes and seemed to fall asleep standing up as the Mole began clapping with emotion written all over his face. Otter joined in and the Rat had his hands raised to do likewise when the Badger said, "Just a moment."

The Badger clasped *his* hands on his head and said: "We're still with you while, according to you, you're still on the other side of the water. Carry on."

"Well," said Toad, "I travelled through woods and glades, skirting fields along hedgerows, keeping well out of sight and shying away from any evidence of habitation until at last I breasted a hilly copse and found myself overlooking a village – and the sea; the very same sea I must have flown across, I realised with a glow of pride – distant white cliffs were discernable in the sunshine!

"Again I laid low until nightfall, then I crept down into the village and moved stealthily along the waterfront, hoping I might hear a friendly English voice, but I heard nothing but the lapping of waves. My next thought was to steal a boat – borrow a boat, that is – but all of them had been hauled up the beach and each proved too heavy for even me to lug back to the low water mark alone. So there was nothing else for it: I braced myself and set forth to get back to England under my own steam."

The Rat said: "Under your own steam?"

"I *swam* back!" shrieked Toad.

Fully a minute must have gone by after Toad's last words; he spent it strutting up and down, sending the bell ropes swirling around him with gleeful flicks as he waited for applause.

Then the Badger hauled himself to his feet.

"*Flew* there, *swam* back!" he said, looking up a rope to where it disappeared through a hole in the ceiling. "First he's a bird, then he's a fish! *Flew* there, *swam* back! You've certainly surpassed yourself this time, Toad, you've surely done that! I think the knock on the head is the key to it – I don't doubt at all you've had a knock on the head, because you *did* go up and you've undoubtedly come down. But where? Where no one, not even the most skilled of flying men has yet succeeded in reaching? No, no; flew there, swam back, eh? Dear me, with your imagination, Toad, have you ever considered writing a book?"

The Badger addressed the Rat.

"You and Mole see him home, would you, and make sure he has a good tuck-in before you put him to bed; he truly looks worn-out and hungry. I'll have another chat with him when he has completely recovered, poor fellow."

As the Badger made to leave the ringing chamber, accompanied by Otter, he muttered again, "Flew there, swam back!"

He turned at the top of the steps and smiled at Toad.

"And please leave those bells alone, my lad, until you've had at least one lesson! D'you hear?"

\*  \*  \*

The Rat and the Mole departed from Toad Hall leaving its owner sleeping soundly on a full stomach, and borrowed Toad's dinghy to get back to their own residence.

Toad had protested the truth of his story throughout the meal they prepared for him and right until the moment his eyes closed with fatigue.

"Do you believe him, Ratty?" asked the Mole.

"Who's to say?" said the Rat, watching with pleasure the straight wake created by his immaculate sculling.

"What I mean," said the Mole, "is do you think any of it's true – either that he flew across the water or that he swam back?"

"Believe one, it's possible to believe the other," replied the Rat. "If Toad hadn't flown to France he'd have no cause to attempt to swim back, would he? And that's been done more than once, the swim – by dedicated men who spent months, perhaps years, training; it's twenty miles or so, and Toad never was one for keeping himself in the pink. Still, when you're desperate . . . But *flew* there?"

"O, so as Badger says, it could all have been in the imagination after a knock on the head?"

"On the other hand," said the Rat, "there is one piece of undeniable evidence that doesn't fit into place unless . . ."

He lay on his oars and asked the Mole: "It couldn't have escaped you – the smell on Toad's breath whenever you went near him?"

"Er, yes," said the Mole uneasily. "I didn't like mentioning it, but it was overpoweringly strong and –"

"Garlic!" said the Rat.

"Of course!" said the Mole . "The stuff *you* like – but takes my appetite away . . . just as Toad indicated it did *his*."

"Garlic!" repeated the Rat. "I know how much Toad hates it, always has; whenever he came round to my place for dinner I had to deny myself the pleasure of it. He positively abominated that delectable root and nothing, absolutely nothing – I'm certain – would induce him to allow any substance even suggestive of it to approach his lips; unless it was the direct pangs of hunger."

The Rat sculled on, the Mole sat pensive.

"O my, it makes you wonder," the Mole said at last.

"It does that," said the Rat.

They were almost home before either of them spoke again.

"Ratty, do you think Toad will ever change?" asked the Mole.

A mallard emerging from the reeds at that moment emitted a raucous burst of laughter that echoed along the River Bank, a torrent of derision that only a duck can achieve, as if it had overheard the question.

The Rat grinned at the sound and put a wiggle into the wake.

"I think never, Mole," he said. "At any rate, I for one *hope* old Toady will never change!"

The Mole put both of his paws to his eyes and rubbed them to disguise some emotion or other.

"O I'm so happy you feel that way, Ratty," he said, "for so do I, so very, *very* much so do I!"

# The Water Rat's Ark

FOR THE fourth morning running the Rat and the Mole worked at clearing away snow to give themselves room to move outside their front door – and this morning it was more of a task than ever: no longer just a case of humping the snow to this side or that, for the tops of the sides were now too high to reach; it meant shovelling and scraping and humping it all to tip over onto the ice thickening on the river.

"If it goes on like this we're bound to have a white Christmas," puffed the Mole, in a tone conveying the hope that such would indeed be the case.

"*If* it does," said the Rat, stooping and scooping up a pawful of snow. It was wet and clingy, and the air temperature was not dropping rapidly, as it had done on the three previous days, to freeze it on top of the older snow. So would there be another fall tonight, the Rat wondered, or was the weather pattern about to change?

He sniffed at the sky and breathed an inconclusive "Hmmm."

Christmas was still more than two weeks away and it would be most unusual, he reasoned, if snow arriving this early in December stayed around for that length of time. On the other hand the weather had been unusual, to say the least, ever since the glorious spring's maturing into a scorching summer, the longest in living memory, which had baked the land, drying up reservoirs and streams right until, incredibly,

85

November the ninth – when, as suddenly as a candle flame being snuffed out, the unseasonable heat turned into a black frost.

> *Black frost, long frost;*
> *White frost; three days and then rain.*

The Rat recalled the time-worn saying, which had proved so true. Black frosts had gripped the land all through the remainder of November and until this present December white-out. Another piece of country weather lore had stood the test just as well: *If onion skins be thick and tough, the winter will be cold and rough.* Onion skins had been thick and tough – and the winter could hardly be colder or rougher.

Or could it?

The Rat suddenly acted as if irritated. He frowned and grunted and discarded his shovel by sticking it into the pile of snow, in a manner that clearly said he was doing no more of *that*, thank you!

"Mole," he announced, "I'm going for a stroll: coming or not?"

The Mole, surprised at the Rat's demeanour, replied: "A stroll – *now*? Goodness me, it's hardly strolling weather! Besides we've not yet finished clearing the path and –"

"Please yourself," the Rat said brusquely, at the same time bustling the Mole aside and proceeding determinedly off along the River Bank, sinking in the snow up to his knees and sometimes higher at every step.

"Well, I . . .Well, I'll . . .! Well *blow* it!" exploded the Mole crossly.

He flung down his own shovel to express his annoyance, hurled a couple of snowballs after the departing Rat and shouted "How rude!" each time, then carried on shovelling at twice his previous pace, trying the while to fathom what had come over his friend.

The Rat hadn't intended to be rude and in truth wasn't even aware that he might have been. His thoughts were all of the weather: something about it worried him and though he couldn't pinpoint exactly what the something was, he knew the answer was elusively in the back of his mind.

Perhaps some older and wiser head in the community might jog his memory, he told himself; at any rate, he felt impelled to make the effort to find out.

The first animal he encountered struggling across the winter scene was a rabbit, making hard work of dragging a sledge laden with a bulging sack.

"Hello, good morning!" called the Rat.

"What's good about it?" grumbled the rabbit. "Give us summer all the year round, I say. Why winter was ever invented I'll never understand!"

"Perhaps so we could have spring and autumn in between," suggested the Rat. "But we certainly had an extra ration of sun this year, didn't we? Can't complain about that!"

"We could have done with more rain early on," said the rabbit, who was obviously one of those who, like farmers, refuse to be *absolutely* pleased about anything, "and then the carrots would have been bigger and fatter and would have lasted longer. This here's the second-last sack from my store – how we'll keep body and soul together after they've gone I can't begin to imagine. Still, I should have known – I could see trouble ahead, all the signs were there."

"Were they indeed?" said the Rat. "That interests me greatly: what signs, may I ask?"

"O, signs," said the rabbit.

"Yes, but what signs exactly?" insisted the Rat.

"Just *signs*," said the rabbit, beginning to wish he hadn't tried to appear so wise and knowing, since he'd not seen any significant signs but hadn't thought to be taken up on the matter, "you know – like *Red sky at night, shepherd's delight; Red sky in the morning, shepherd's warning* – that sort of thing. I distinctly remember seeing a red sky some morning or other."

"Hmm," responded the Rat, "but not recently, eh? I was thinking more of –"

"Here's another," the rabbit interrupted, "*Ne'er cast a clout till May is out.* I did – I left my singlet off and caught a cold. Never again though, I'll watch it next year – but is it the blossom or the month has to be out? Never could be sure."

"I had in mind some indication of the weather to follow immediately on this snow," persisted the Rat.

"O did you now?" said the rabbit. "Well, I've got far more

important matters on *my* mind! If I don't get these carrots home soon there'll be no stew on the go for lunch, and I'll have the whole family down on me. So I'll say good-day to you."

The rabbit struggled off with his sledge, but turned after half a dozen strides, obviously feeling he hadn't come up to the Rat's expectations, and called: "What about this? *You may shear your sheep when the elder blossoms peep.* No? O well."

The Rat continued on his way, thinking there'd better be wiser heads in the offing than that of the rabbit if his sortie was to be worthwhile.

A rook approached and circled overhead before gliding down to alight and walk beside him.

"Ooh!" the rook exclaimed as the snow tingled his feet. "It's bad enough walking in this, but I wouldn't manage at all well if I was one of those birds who hopped, would I? Chest

deep in snow after the first hop; imagine: struggle clear, hop, chest-deep! Struggle clear, hop, chest-deep! Struggle clear, hop . . ."

The Rat chuckled at his new companion's good humour.

The rook observed: "I'm surprised to see you, I must say; hardly another soul about for miles. Wouldn't have left the colony myself this morning but I just *had* to stretch my wings.

What has dragged you out in such weather, might I ask?"

"Looking for clues, you could say," the Rat told him. "My friend Mole is hoping for a white Christmas. What's your opinion?"

"O dear, not easy, that one; a tricky question indeed any year. Talking about signposts, aren't we? Yes . . .tricky, Let's see now: the only time we rooks stayed feeding close to home this year – before the onset of winter, that is – instead of roaming far and wide from our nests was the day – but *you'll* remember – it was the day of what we've all come to think of as Toad's storm. That was the only storm last summer and none of us will forget it, will we? Least of all Toad! The blackbirds were unusually shrill that evening – so were the woodpeckers; they knew as well as we that the weather was about to break up. So did the spiders, I recall, spinning very short webs or not bothering to spin at all.

"But a white Christmas, eh? None of *that* seems to help, does it? I wonder if there was a clue in the behaviour of the cuckoos this year?"

"It was different from normal?" asked the Rat.

"Very much so," said the rook. "You couldn't have been paying much attention last spring otherwise it would have struck you. You're conversant, I take it, with the rhyme:

> *The cuckoo comes in April,*
> *He sings his song in May;*
> *In the middle of June he changes tune*
> *And in July he flies away.*

That's invariably the routine with cuckoos – so what made them decide to arrive in May this year, not sing until June and not leave until August?"

"Is that a fact?" said the Rat. "Now that certainly is food for thought – though I'm not sure what to think about it."

"Hope it helps," said the rook, "but ooh, my feet *are* cold now – and speaking of food . . ."

With that he launched into the air, leaving the Rat to ponder alone on the significance, if any, of the cuckoo evidence.

It was fully ten minutes before the Rat came across anyone

else to talk to. He had paused to rest in the lee of a beech tree and a voice called: "Care for a nut or two to keep your strength up, traveller? O, it's you, Mr Rat! How about some refreshment?"

The Rat looked up and saw a pair of bright eyes set above chewing cheeks, peering down at him from a lower branch.

"Hello, young squirrel!" he responded. "How kind of you – a cup of something hot would be welcome."

"Just this minute brewed a pot," said the squirrel, "give me a sec."

He disappeared into the trees and reappeared alongside the

Rat – albeit more than a second later but not much more – with a tray of wholemeal biscuits on a plate and two cups of steaming tea with not a drop spilt in the saucers.

"Hope it's to your liking, sir," he said. "It's my favourite flavour."

It needed only a sniff and a confirmatory sip for the Rat to pronounce appreciatively: "Orange Pekoe – a very superior tea, I've always thought."

"Thank you," said the squirrel happily, "it's so nice entertaining an animal of taste. But may I ask why you're floundering around in these frozen wastes? Nothing amiss, I hope?"

"Nothing amiss, nothing yet, at any rate," said the Rat. "It's just that . . . well, let me ask you: what are your thoughts about the present cold spell – in view of what's gone before, I mean?"

"Ah, as a matter of fact I've been giving the weather lots of thought," said the squirrel. "Something a waxwing told me sticks in my mind; I met him the day he flew in from Scandinavia *at the end of August*. 'Good gracious,' I said to him, really surprised I was, 'what on earth are you doing here at this time of the year?' And he told me, 'I've come much earlier than usual expecting the severest of weather.'"

"He said that, did he? Well, we had a long time to wait for it if he meant this snow. I assume he *was* referring to snow?"

"He wasn't specific, I'm afraid," said the squirrel. "But I'll give you a fact that must have a bearing on the matter: this year's walnut crop was *bumper* – I could've filled two larders from floor to ceiling, never mind just the one. And that, sir, meant only one thing: the weather was going to be *strange*."

The Rat took his leave of the squirrel, much impressed by that hospitable animal's interpretation of the nut glut. Who, after all, could know better about nuts than a squirrel? The weather had *been* strange, was *still* strange. The question was: might it get any stranger?

Racking his mind for the clue he knew was lurking there the Rat pressed on, thinking at one moment he might even knock up the Badger to seek his counsel, and then thinking that indeed he might not, in view of the Badger's antipathy to being disturbed at such time of the year; and before he knew it he was outside the gates of Toad Hall – so he went in.

Toad stood with his back to a roaring log fire in the drawing room, and though he greeted the Rat politely and made room for him near the fire, his manner was aloof, as if he and his closest friend were now on different levels. But the Rat knew that Toad had adopted this attitude with all of his friends, the Badger included, since his flying machine escapade.

Toad wasn't putting on a superior air; he was feeling sorry for himself. It was his "I'm very hurt but suffering in noble silence" mask of admonishment for their not acknowledging and treating him as a hero. For though no one had actually told him they totally disbelieved the tale of his pioneering flight across the Channel, it was the way they all said, "Yes, Toad, yes – we believe you" that suggested they didn't really.

His friends could hardly be blamed for this, for nothing had ever appeared in the newspapers even hinting that his story could be true. Everyone hoped Toad would soon revert to being his old self again – even nettling them with some new outlandish pursuit would be a welcome sign – but the return to normality was taking longer than expected.

Pretending not to notice Toad's manner the Rat said: "So glad I found you at home, Toady, I need your help; what old sayings about the weather can you recall?"

"Sayings about the weather?" Toad repeated vaguely, allowing his gaze to wander to the window. "What sayings about the weather?"

"*Sayings!*" repeated the Rat. "You know – such as your corns are tingling or your rheumatism's playing up so it's going to be wet – that sort of thing."

"I haven't any corns and rheumatism's never played me up, wet or dry," said Toad.

"Come on," insisted the Rat, "you know full well what I mean. You must remember some weather wisdom your Toad ancestors handed down. Think! It's very important."

"O, very important, eh?" Toad's voice took on an interested note. "Toad sayings? About the weather? Mmmm . . . let's see, yes – here's one: *A wind from the east maltreats Toad and beast*. How's that?"

"That's good – that's fine: Just the kind of thing I'm after. How clever of you. Any others?"

"Clever? O yes, of course," said Toad, beginning to puff up. "Must be masses of others – Toads always knew what was what and all were gifted with words; naturally these qualities were handed down to me. Listen:

> *If the sun goes pale to bed*
> *Tomorrow's sky will be like lead."*

"Go on!" urged the Rat.

> *"The cock went crowing to bed*
> *So he'll rise with a watery head."*

"More! More!" cried the Rat.

> *"I saw a blackbird singing in a lower branch*
> *With his tail straight down – waiting to shoot the*
> *water off."*

"When – when was that?" demanded the Rat.

"Don't know *when*, just know it as a *saying!*" yelled Toad, feeling so important he began pacing up and down rapidly.

"Go on, then, go on!" exhorted the Rat.

"*The soot fell down my chimney!*" shouted Toad. "That's dampness and wet coming upon us. *The smoke from my fire didn't go straight up, it came swirling down!* Wetness and damp!"

"Keep on, keep going!" shouted the Rat.

Toad declaimed at the ceiling, with ringing conviction:

> *"Be it dry or be it wet,*
> *The weather always pays its debt."*

And he became feverish, running up and down instead of merely pacing up and down, hurling other prophesies into the air as further evidence of the wisdom of the Toads, although the Rat, had he still been paying attention, would have had no difficulty in recognising they were the common property of all country dwellers; such as: *Easter in snow, Christmas in mud; Christmas in snow, Easter in mud;* and: *If birds sing in January, frosts are on the way*; and *Ice in November to bear a duck, the rest of winter's slush and muck.*

But the Rat was no longer listening. He had walked to the window and was gazing out over the white wilderness.

"*That* was it!" he said softly. "That is *it!*"

He turned with a serious expression to Toad, who was still showing remarkable powers of recall, chasing up just about every old saying ever coined.

"You can stop now, Toad, and thank you: you've done it."

"Done it? Done what?" said Toad.

"Told me what I wanted to know. And now we'll have to work really fast, no time to lose, not even a minute."

Toad seemed to deflate an inch or two.

"Er, *work*, you said? Did you say *we'll* have to *work*? Well, I don't think I –"

"I'll rush back and get Mole and as many tools as we can carry; you go and round up Otter and bring all his and your axes and saws and stout ropes to the Wild Wood – we'll be waiting for you there. And hurry, you understand, hurry for pity's sake."

"I don't understand at all!" Toad protested shrilly. "Why should we all be going to the Wild Wood with axes and saws on a day like this?"

"To build what might be termed an ark," the Rat called as he ran out of Toad Hall.

And as he began the struggle back home to recruit the Mole to his plan, the words of Toad that had brought about such a blinding revelation pulsed over and over again through his mind: *Be it dry or be it wet, the weather always pays its debt.*

"Ratty," Toad shouted after him, "do you mean an ark like Noah's?"

But the Rat was out of earshot.

\*   \*   \*

"Don't you see, Mole?" the Rat said as he applied a whetstone vigorously to the cutting edge of an axe, "we're in for a deluge the like of which has never been seen – certainly not in our time. All those parched months with the trees and the grass and the flowers and the crops – even the River itself – thirsting for the water due to them; all this snow is merely a preliminary instalment; when the weather repays its debt in full it'll be all at one go – water owed that will be measured in feet of rain, not just inches. The snow will melt at the same time, all the way back up there (the Rat waved his arm in the direction of upstream) and neither the earth nor the River will be able to cope with it all. I can feel it in my blood, Mole – we are only hours away from being confronted with this terrifying situation."

"Well, you may well be right," said the Mole, busily filing sharp the teeth of a two-handed saw, "I don't doubt it because you usually are; but we have a boat and Toad has several boats and Otter can look after himself in any amount of water and –"

"And Badger and all the other Wild Wooders?" said the Rat. "What kind of boatmen are weasels and stoats and ferrets and squirrels and hedgehogs and the rest? How many rabbits, for instance, have you seen sculling on the River? No, none at all, of course, my friend. So that's why we are heading for the Wild Wood: that's where the timber is to build our ark and that's where the ark will be needed. Shall we be on our way at once?"

\*　　\*　　\*

To the Rat's surprise and relief Otter and Toad were waiting for them at the edge of the Wild Wood.

"I was with you, Ratty, all the way as soon as Toad mentioned 'ark'," explained Otter. "It convinced me of what I'd begun to fear myself – we're really in for it this time. Who's going to rouse Badger?"

"No need for that yet, I think," said the Rat. "Let him sleep a few hours longer while we get on with the task in hand. Really it's not so much an ark we're after – that would be too tall an order at this stage; just a raft, as big as we can manage: a dozen of these elms should be enough and we can use the branches to build a shelter on it. Agreed? Let's go to work then."

Soon the sound of axes hacking at wood was carrying for miles around on the chill air. The first elm was chipped and ready for the saw when the first Wild Wooder showed himself – a stoat snuggled up in his white winter coat and hardly visible against the snowy background, except for his eyes and the black tip of his tail.

"*What are you doing?* " he demanded in an angry squeak. "What *do* you *think* you are *doing?*"

Without waiting for an answer he vanished: but the Rat and the Mole had barely taken up position at the ends of their two-handed saw to bring the elm down, when the stoat reappeared – with a score more of his kind, their eyes glinting red with anger.

"Stop it! Stop it! Stop it!" they shrieked in a chorus that soon was swelled by hundreds more voices as cohorts of weasel and stoat reinforcements, backed up by ferrets and hedgehogs, mice and squirrels and all manner of other Wild Wood residents, rushed to the scene.

The Rat and Otter shouted in vain to make themselves heard above the din, and the mob began pressing in close, jostling the Mole and Toad and seizing and wielding axes and saws in a very threatening manner.

If the Chief Weasel hadn't pushed his way through to the front the situation could have become very serious. Not that there was any sign of friendliness on *his* face as he glared at the Rat and demanded: "What is the meaning of this criminal and unprovoked assault on our territory?"

"It's not an assault!" protested the Rat. "Just the reverse, in fact: we're here to rescue you – it's a mission of mercy."

"Don't listen to him," squeaked a very belligerent ferret, shaking both fists, "we are being attacked, no mistake!"

The Chief Weasel asked: "What kind of mercy mission could deliberately try to deprive us of the roofs over our heads in weather like this? The only rescuing *we* need is from the likes of *you* – you vandals!"

"Listen to me," pleaded the Rat, "I just know we're about to have a flood the like of which has never been seen and it will take twelve of your trees to build an ark and –"

His explanation was drowned by screams of rage and a phalanx of weasels and stoats kept him and his River Bank companions at bay while the others moved in, picked up the remaining axes and saws and tools and ropes and vanished among the trees with them; then the rearguard Wild Wooders also withdrew, leaving the River Bankers in an apparently helpless situation.

"What now?" whispered Toad when everything was quiet

again. "Do we forget all about it and go home?"

"We can't do that," pointed out Otter, "nothing's changed – what Ratty and I feel is going to happen is still going to happen."

"It's time to awaken Badger," said the Rat.

"How can we possibly?" argued Toad. "If we go into the Wild Wood that lot waiting in the undergrowth will whack us right out again – with axes!"

But the Mole said: "We needn't go *through* the Wild Wood – we can go *under* it."

"Under it? O, how preposterous, Mole!" said Toad. "It may be all right for tunnelers such as you, but *I'm* not digging my –"

"Mole, you're right, you splendid fellow," said the Rat, "you've remembered, haven't you – how we left Badger's house after your first visit?"

"Of course!" said Otter. "Badger brought the three of us along one of his secret bolt-holes to the very edge of the Wild Wood. But where did we come out?"

"Just over there, unless I'm very much mistaken," said the Mole, indicating a tangle of bramble creepers trailing over an outcrop of rocks near the roots of a tree.

He went across and carefully pulled aside the brambles and the brushwood and dried leaves caught up in them – and exposed the entrance to a tunnel.

"It's a very long tunnel I recall," he informed the others, "also very dark, and this time we've no lantern to light the way. But I'm used to this sort of thing, as you know, so if I go first and you all stay close in line behind with a hand on the shoulder of the one ahead, we'll get through all right. And Ratty – please remember to pull the brambles and brushwood back into place after us; Badger's bound to want reassurance about that."

The Mole stepped confidently into the passageway with his friends in tow like a string of barges, and soon they were enveloped in total blackness, the air damp around them. On and on they went, the tunnel dipping and winding, and to Toad, the only one who hadn't passed this way before, it seemed they would never reach the end. He began emitting small whimpers and gulps – though he bravely tried to hold

97

them back – indicating he was in some distress at being confined in so dark and narrow a space.

Otter, who was immediately in front, and the Rat, who was behind, comforted and encouraged him – the Otter by patting Toad's paw trembling on his shoulder, the Rat by squeezing

Toad's shoulder as it quivered in his grasp, both of them appreciating that it was no mean thing for such a totally open-air creature as he to endure this claustrophobic ordeal.

All were immensely relieved when at last the Mole said: "There's a glimmer of light ahead – coming from under Badger's back door, I shouldn't wonder; as we get nearer I'll start calling out to assure him it's only his friends arriving."

A few moments later the Mole was shouting: "Badger, Badger – don't be alarmed, it's only us your friends, Ratty, Otter, Toad and me; I'm Mole. Badger, Badger – don't be alarmed, it's only us your friends, Ratty, Otter, Toad and me; I'm Mole . . ."

By which time the procession had reached the door – and it soon became obvious that though the sound of Mole's voice had penetrated its oaken thickness, its message had not. The door was flung back and in the blinding light the Badger stood scowling and pointing a double-barrel shotgun.

"Back, you vermin!" he commanded. "You would dare beard a Badger in his sett?"

Then he realised blinkingly who was calling on him.

"Well, I never – I was about to start out to join you lot; fancy you turning up like this along one of my bolt-holes – I hope no one spotted you. Come in, come in; you've time for a mug of mulled ale now you're here before we proceed to put matters right outside."

It was the Rat's turn to be surprised.

"You say you were coming to join us, Badger? You *knew* something had happened outside?"

"Of course," said the Badger. "I may sleep longer than most when the mood takes me but absolutely nothing goes on in the Wild Wood I don't quickly hear about. You want to build an ark, I understand, and they won't let you?"

"Why, yes, but –"

"That's what the hedgehog said; and you're convinced we're in for a flood the like of which hasn't been seen before, Ratty?"

"I am indeed, Badger, and I'll tell you why –"

"I take your word for it," said the Badger. "You agree, Otter? Yes, well it wouldn't become the likes of me to question the instinct of water creatures such as you, any more than it does them out there."

At that moment a shower of soot fell down the chimney, almost dousing the fire and sending smoke billowing into the room.

"That's the third time in the last half-hour," said the Badger, wafting the smoke away from his nose.

Toad said eagerly: "That means dampness and wet, Badger! It's a sign only we Toads are aware of. It was actually I who let Ratty know through a secret Toad saying – that we were going to be flooded, isn't that so, Ratty?"

Before the Badger could say, "Toad, *everyone* knows that sign," which is what he intended to say, the Rat said: "I'm thankful to you, Toad – and the entire neighbourhood will be soon, I hope."

The Badger gave the Rat a knowing look as he said: "Good lad, Toad. Now then, Ratty, how long have we got, eh?"

"Only a matter of hours, in my view, once the rain starts," said the Rat.

"Drink up your ale then and we'll make a move," said the Badger.

"Do you think you ought to gather up some of your valuables before we go, Badger, just in case we can't get back down here?" suggested Otter.

"Nothing's to be valued more than the saving of a single life," said the Badger, "so I'll take only my 12-bore and a cartridge or two to emphasise the point to any out there who may hold a differing view. Actually the cartridges are only blanks – but they won't know that."

In a clearing just a hundred yards from his front door, where the snow was comparatively shallow because so much had collected on the branches of a holly tree, the Badger announced: "We won't waste time seeking them, we'll bring them here."

He pointed his shotgun up at the holly branches and squeezed the trigger. Snow disturbed by the bang cascaded down; not icy hard chunks, the Rat noted, but wet chunks that sploshed against whoever or whatever they dropped on. Had the tide turned? he wondered. Had the thaw already begun?

"That'll fetch 'em," observed the Badger, ejecting the spent cartridge.

A weasel showed himself – and vanished as soon as he laid eyes on the Badger.

Then in seconds, hundreds of faces appeared all around; sharp and mean faces, sullen and resentful faces, silently watching. The Mole moved in closer to his friends.

Making great show of placing a new cartridge in his shotgun the Badger ordered in a voice that brooked no disobedience: "Fetch the Chief Weasel!"

The ranks of watchers began parting to allow their leader, who had obviously been waiting on developments from a safe distance, to come to the front. He indicated as he stepped uncertainly into the open that he wished his escape route through the crowd to be kept open, then looked sideways at the Badger and said cautiously: "Yes?"

The Badger didn't beat about the bush.

"Bring back all those tools you stole!" he said.

The Chief Weasel caught his breath.

"*Stole*, is it? Huh! That's a fine thing coming from one who sets himself up as a pillar of society! It's easy to see why creatures like *them* (he shook a fist at the Badger's companions) think they can take liberties with the likes of *us* when leading lights like *you* turn a blind eye to the truth! (His supporters gave voice in a loud cheer). Not *stole*, Mr Badger, that's not the word for what we did; *confiscated* is what it amounts to, nothing more or less, in order to save our homes from *their* vandalism. Do you know what they were up to, these River Bank friends of yours? If you'd been there, as I was – as *we* were (chorus of Wild Wood encouragement as he encompassed them with a wave) you'd have seen them carrying out a vicious onslaught on our environment. Just because our ways are different from theirs is no reason for them to –"

There was a bang as the Badger discharged another cartridge into the air, and even more chunks of soggy snow avalanched onto heads.

"Pay attention," the Badger said, "there is little enough time left. The creatures accused of being vicious vandals, these friends of mine *and* yours from the River Bank could, if they so wished, walk away from here now with clear consciences, having made an heroic and utterly selfless attempt to save me and all of you, my fellow Wild Wooders, from the impending calamity which they are convinced is threatening this land.

(The Chief Weasel brushed away a big drop of moisture, which he assumed to be melted snow, that splashed on his forehead and ran down his nose.)

"I share my friend's apprehension," continued the Badger. "Their sixth sense tells them the rains are coming, make no mistake: that the rain due to us is on its way, all of it, all at one go, an enormous volume of water that will sweep everything before it. My own sixth sense tells me that their sixth sense is right.

101

(More heavy drops splashed on the Chief Weasel and everyone else and faces began turning upwards with worried expressions.)

"Ask yourselves one question, those among you who still doubt the good intention of the Rat, the Mole, the Otter and Toad. It is this: Who here needs have the least fear of any flood? And the answer is, of course, he who owns a boat or is completely at home in the water. The Rat and the Mole have a boat; Toad has more than one boat; Otter, you might say, is a boat unto himself. But you animals – could you muster even a leaky tin bath among you?"

The Chief Weasel flicked at another heavy splash of water that spattered his cheek and said, but with a noticeable lack of conviction: "All this talk of floods . . .when obviously we're going to have a white Christmas."

To everyone's surprise Toad then stepped in front of the Badger, raised his arms as if invoking the wrath of Heaven and intoned in a voice of doom: "Hear me, my brethren, for I am sent this fateful day to impart to you the wisdom of the ancient Toads; to reveal to you the secret known only to Toads since time began and jealously guarded and handed down from father to son through the generations; hear it now and heed it, ignore its message at your peril: *Be it dry or be it wet, the weather always pays its debt.* I have spoken!"

As Toad finished speaking he allowed his arms to drop – and there was another loud bang. Everyone looked to the Badger's gun – and saw that it had nothing to do with this bang: the Badger was in the act of replacing the previous spent cartridge. Almost immediately a torrent of water descended on the clearing, bringing with it most of the snow still clinging to the holly tree.

"That was a clap of thunder – and the rain has begun in earnest," the Badger said loudly, adding in just as loud an aside to the River Bankers, "let us go now, gentlemen, and see to our boats."

He turned and started out of the clearing through the quickly parting ranks of stoats and weasels, and the Rat and Mole and Toad and Otter, taking their cue, followed as he headed resolutely into the trees, apparently leaving the now uncertain Wild Wooders to their fate.

"Well done, Toad!" the Badger called over his shoulder when they were out of earshot of those in the clearing, "a brilliantly timed intervention on your part; if that doesn't move them nothing will. One way or another you're certainly the hero of the hour."

Toad seemed to grow six inches all round at the Badger's words; the Mole, on the other hand, turned with a look of disbelief to the Rat behind him. But the Rat merely responded with a small smile and a shake of his head to discourage any audible comment from his friend.

"I'll wager," the Badger went on, "that by the time we reach the edge of the woods where you attempted to begin building your ark, all your tools and more will be awaiting us – plus a lot of willing helpers."

And so proved to be the case.

The army of Wild Wooders who had acted so obstructively at the same spot earlier were now lined up submissively, many of them holding axes and saws and many others carrying candle lanterns – for darkness had descended early even for a December afternoon. The lantern tops steamed in the rain, which had now become a downpour of tropical proportions.

The Chief Weasel again stood at the front of his clan, panting from the effort of getting there ahead of the Badger, whom he proceeded to address meekly but urgently: "Thanks to the wisdom of Mr Toad and yourself, sir, we have come to realise the truth of the situation. All my people are willing and anxious to carry out each and every instruction you and your friends give in order to bring about the speedy building of the ark that may save us. Tell us how now, sir, and we'll begin."

\*　　\*　　\*

A cry of "Timmm-berrr!" heralded the fall of the first of the elms, and teams at work on felling others earmarked for the raft paused and held their lanterns aloft to view the spectacle.

No animal derives any pleasure from seeing a tree, so majestically beautiful, so accommodating, so strong and yet so helpless, being cut down in its prime. And although on this occasion it was such a desperate necessity to do just that, the Rat, like most others present, still felt a stab of sadness when

103

the gentle giant groaned as it toppled and smashed its branches to the ground with what sounded like a dying gasp.

But today there was no time for sorrowing. In an instant a horde of weasels and stoats had set upon the fallen elm, hacking and rasping at its limbs with axes and saws; and even the raw, rough noises they made in the process were almost drowned by the roar of the rain.

The rain was unbelievable: it came down in thick, continuous sheets as if aimed by some force intent on scourging the Earth. It was warm rain, moreover, and the drenched animals hastening to prepare the ark floundered and slithered as the snow, which had been so deep at the start, melted into a slippery floor of ice that in turn was soon transformed into a sea of mud.

No wind drove the rain, no lightning accompanied the thunder. These elements, the Rat suspected as instinctively as he had expected the rain, were being held in abeyance for a terrifying climactic onslaught.

On and on into the night and all the way through it the frenzy of preparation continued non-stop. As soon as a tree had been toppled and its branches lopped, the Herculean task began of hauling it over the ground to lie close to the one made ready earlier – a task that became ever more back-breaking, of course, as the distance between the raft taking shape and the next tree in line increased.

The Rat, supervising the lashing together of the trunks as well as helping with the sawing and axing, asked the Mole as they took their turn yet again on either end of a two-handed saw: "Have you seen Toad around lately?"

The Mole flicked a finger in the direction of Toad Hall. The Rat looked and saw that the Hall was lit up.

"The lights went on nearly an hour ago," said the Mole, offering no interpretation.

"O, Toady, how could you!" the Rat said under his breath as they began sawing.

At first light, grey as it was and with the unrelenting downpour almost obliterating the view, an exhausted Mole nudged the Rat and pointed again towards Toad Hall, still lit up, but this time drawing attention to a new development: the River had risen so high it was lapping over the edge of

Toad's lawn rising away from its farther bank; more alarmingly it was welling out over the lower-lying water meadow on the nearer bank, inching rapidly towards the Wild Wood.

"And still three more trees needed, Ratty," said the Mole. "Can we possibly cope?"

"We can – by working *twice* as hard, *three* times as hard, *four* times as hard!" replied the Rat, rushing to the tenth elm and swinging his axe.

The water had actually crept to the raft itself as the twelfth and final tree was being manhandled into position and the ropes hauled on and knotted to secure it there. And still there was the sheltering cabin to be constructed.

"Quickly! *Quickly!*" the Rat exhorted them all as they set about it – and took upon himself the job of bending one end of the longest and stoutest hawser available to a corner of the raft, climbing the nearest oak tree with the other end and tying it around the trunk and the lowest branch.

This achieved, he paused to survey the scene around – and caught his breath.

Upstream the entire landscape was now nothing but a seascape dotted with island shapes as far as the eye could see. Even as he watched, some of the islands vanished, others seemed to be on the move – in this direction. At right-angles to the Wild Wood the meadows were so inundated that the raft was being lifted and the water was deeply into the Wood itself; downstream the lawn of Toad Hall was no longer visible, nor even the windows of the ground floor, and in the blink of an eye a light that had still gleamed from the first floor went out.

"O, my goodness, Toad!" the Rat said in anguish, as he lowered himself from the tree.

He had to drop into the water and haul himself along the hawser to reach the raft, now loaded with Wild Wooders of all description packing into the cabin while some stalwarts were still hammering nails into it.

The Badger stretched out a paw to help the Rat aboard.

"D'you think that rope will hold us if the rush of water becomes really strong?" he shouted above the clamour and the banging and the drumming of the rain.

"The rope should," said the Rat, "but I'm not sure about the tree – it's very old; the rope wasn't long enough to reach to any other."

"Uh-huh. Now – where's Toad?" the Badger asked. "No one seems to have clapped eyes on him for hours."

The Rat reluctantly nodded towards Toad Hall.

"He may have returned home, Badger, I fear."

"Never!" said the Badger. "Surely not . . ."

He stared at the Hall, became silent and then clutched the Rat's arm.

"Do my eyes deceive me, or do you see what I see?"

The Rat *did* see what the Badger saw: Toad in a dinghy, splashing and rolling a great deal but sculling determinedly towards the raft against the fast-flowing floodwater. What was more, he had in tow a punt so heavily laden with something or other that it was almost awash.

"Good heavens, what on earth's he up to?" said the Badger. "Surely he'll never make it to here, Ratty?"

"Not without help," observed the Rat, diving into the water without another word and swimming swiftly with the current.

He reached the dinghy in hardly any time at all and said as he hauled himself inboard: "Give me the oars and sit back, Toad, I'll do the rest. What's all that in the punt?"

"Supplies, of course," replied the Toad, "food! No one else thought of bringing any, did they? Seems I have to think of *everything*, Ratty!"

Even the Rat found the rowing hard going, as the punt was shipping water from above and below and was on the verge of sinking when at last it was near enough to the raft for willing hands to reach out and hold it alongside.

"At the double now," Toad ordered, "get my supplies transferred before they go to the bottom; we may have nothing else to eat for weeks – this could even be your Christmas dinner!"

Toad had brought all manner of provisions from his larder, which must surely have been more akin to a warehouse. There were tins of tongue in jelly, game pies and veal and ham pies; whole Stilton and Wensleydale cheeses and two big wheels of Dutch Gouda; two geese newly-cooked, two hams newly-boiled, dozens and dozens of eggs newly-hard-boiled and still warm; box after box of plain and fancy biscuits; cartons of *marrons glacés* and jars of peaches in brandy, tray upon tray of chocolate peppermints and bottles of lemonade and lime juice by the score.

All were somehow made room for in the cabin, although a number of the younger Wild Wooders, wet as they were on their outsides, lost no time in storing a quantity of lemonade on their insides.

Heavy thunder accompanied Toad's arrival on the raft, this time preceded by spectacular lightning, and the Wild Wooders regarded him with awe as he moved among them benignly patting a small head here and a small head there, offering words of comfort and encouragement and popping chocolate peppermint creams into open mouths.

Outside the cabin the storm grew wilder, the water rose; a gale was springing up and the Rat and Otter watched anxiously as the raft, now nearly branch-high to the Wild Wood, tugged and heaved and strained at the oak tree, anchoring it as a cavalcade of objects at the mercy of the flood, things such as garden sheds and wheelbarrows, barrels and boxes, chicken coops, farm carts and whole haystacks, went rushing by.

Suddenly the raft lurched, as if the retaining hawser had parted; it was not the hawser, however, but the old tree that had succumbed to the force of the water. Its great clump of tired roots reared into the air like the tentacles of some sea monster, then lashed back on the bubbling surface – and tree and raft in harness joined the helpless cavalcade.

"We'll probably end up way out at sea, you realise, Ratty?" said Otter.

An unseen hand seemed to clutch the raft from below and interrupt its momentum for a second or two – probably the branches of a smaller tree, it occurred to the Rat – and the oak overtook it. The raft was buffeted free and flung to the side, and it and the oak, still tethered, continued their flight on parallel courses a hawser's length apart. It was fortunate for everyone that this happened.

The raft was carried down the front of Toad Hall, the oak down the rear; the hawser stretched itself across the gable end

*The raft was carried down the front of Toad Hall.*

and was arrested; and raft and oak, after smashing against top floor windows on both sides, nestled close to the house.

The thunder cracked louder, the lightning flashed brighter and the water inched even higher. But hour after hour the Hall kept its hold on them.

Toad spent all the time in the cabin, urging meats and sweetmeats upon his willing audience as he regaled them with tale after tale illustrating the wisdom of the Toads, who (it now transpired, becoming public knowledge for the first time) had actually given Noah himself the nod and the wink that he'd better waste not even one more minute in getting on with *his* ark.

"I'm not saying we are in for forty days and forty nights of rain now," said Toad, "but on the other hand I'm not saying we're *not*. (*These meaningless words seemed to impress and comfort his audience greatly*.) I've so many Toad sayings stored away in this old head of mine that often it's very hard work and very tiring sifting through them to find exactly the right one; but it's in there somewhere, I assure you, and I'll let you know when I find it, just as I did to guide old Ratty. What a blessing he sought my help!"

Outside the cabin, as night fell, the Rat keeping watch alone noticed a slackening in the rain and a fading in the thunder; he'd seen no lightning for fifteen minutes. At last the storm peak was over, he assessed with relief. Behind him in the cabin even Toad's voice was now silenced, and an orchestra of snores high, low and middle-range was performing in unrehearsed concert.

The Rat sat in a hunch against the cabin wall, rested his head on raised knees and sighed thankfully into the deepest of sleeps.

He remained in that position until long after dawn, so exhausted had he been by the strenuous efforts of yesterday, and it wasn't the morning light that roused him but the sudden cessation of movement by the raft, as if it had been jerked still.

A heartening sight greeted him: the water had subsided during the night even more quickly than it had risen during the day and was draining across the lawn of Toad Hall to the River, now rapidly resuming normal proportions. The air smelt of mud, and not surprising, for mud was everywhere and soon was caking young Wild Wooders up to their armpits as they jumped from the raft and splashed about in the receding water, just as any youngster is lured to stamping about in a rain puddle.

Toad emerged, looked up at Toad Hall, peered into windows and seemed not to care at all about the chaos inside, not even when he opened the front doors and a wall of water trapped behind them swept him down his own steps and deposited him in a muddy heap on his lawn. He sat laughing!

The Chief Weasel was among those who rushed to help Toad to his feet and then to inform him loudly for all to hear: "Mr Toad, all of our homes will now be in all kinds of a state, but none more so than yours, there being so much more of it. In gratitude for the wisdom, courage and generosity shown by you on our behalf, I am deeply honoured to pledge that we of the Wild Wood will devote ourselves to setting your home to rights even before we tackle our own. In our eyes, sir, you are a hero!"

Toad beamed and waved in a regal sort of way in acknowledgement of the Wild Wooders' cheering endorsement of their leader's words.

And the Badger, who had watched and listened with a look of amused satisfaction, turned to the Rat and shook his paw with a pressure conveying much more than usual warmth.

"Thank you, Ratty, you *clever* animal for *everything* you've done for us *all*."

\* \* \*

"I think it most unfair," the Mole said, as he and the Rat slipped and slithered through the mud on their way home, "*you* see the danger looming, *you* put yourself at risk to save everyone – and Toad gets all the credit. What gratitude! Disgraceful, I call it! You should have heard him going on and on in that cabin – so boastful, and everyone fawning upon him; I'm so angry!"

The Rat shrugged and smiled.

"All that's important, Mole, is that no one got hurt – isn't it now? And Toad did, after all, remember the old saying *my* grandfather had passed on to me but which I couldn't recall.

And he *did* put himself out to provide all those victuals – and who else remembered that?"

"It's still not fair, Ratty; you deserve a medal and nobody but me seems to know it."

"Come now, my friend, Badger for one knows the truth and Otter for another; that makes three – and reward enough for me. Lots of people who deserve medals never get them, I'm sure, and I daresay some people who get medals never deserved them; that's life. Supposing, for instance, Toad really was the first to fly a machine across the Channel – he'd have earned a medal, wouldn't he? So suppose then, the way things work out, he got his medal for it only today! Toady's the type who needs medals; and at any rate he's his old self again without doubt and that's exactly what we've all been hoping for."

They slipped and slithered on towards home, the Mole silent and obviously extremely thoughtful.

"I suppose you're right again, Ratty," he said eventually. "How *selfless* you are."

"No, no, not at all," protested the Rat with an embarrassed wave of a paw, but a moment later he groaned and the Mole breathed a heartfelt "O my!" as they reached home and saw what the flood had done.

The place was in a dreadful mess: furniture swilled from one room to another, crockery smashed and scattered about, linen and bedding soaked, walls, floors and carpets muddied and reeking, and food sloshed with the mud everywhere, including ceilings.

"Well," said the Rat, "it's no more than we could have expected; but look on the bright side, my friend."

"Bright side?" said the Mole. "*What* bright side, for goodness sake, Ratty?"

"Ask yourself," said the Rat, "when spring comes, as it assuredly will because it always does, what won't we have to do because we'll have done it all for Christmas?"

The Mole thought and thought until the answer dawned on him.

"O *that* bright side, of *course!*" he exclaimed. "'There'll be no spring cleaning at all to do next springtime!"

In no time at all he had armed himself with bucket and

broom and floorcloth, and was setting about the mopping up. And as he worked he suddenly burst into song:

> "A boat makes you stand up and sing,
> For all of the pleasure it bring.
> It's a much nimbler craft
> Than a clumsy old raft,
> Ting-a-ling, ting-a-ling, ting-a-ling."

He turned and saw the Rat looking at him open-mouthed, delight shining from his eyes.

"Do you like that, Ratty?" the Mole asked shyly. "I know that *For all of the pleasure it bring* isn't quite right, but I was hoping you might give me a little help there as you're so good at rhyming; also I haven't thought of a proper last line yet so I just put in three ting-a-lings for now."

"Like it?" said the Rat, hooting with pleasure, "why it's the nicest verse in the whole song; I couldn't do half as well, dear Mole! Let's sing it together . . .

> A boat makes you stand up and sing,
> For all of the pleasure it bring . . ."

They sang verse after verse and chorus after chorus so happily that anyone would have thought spring was already at the door, ringing to be let in.

THE END.